S0-AYX-451

CONTENTS

"Good literature is not a question of forms new or old, but of ideas that must pour freely from the author's heart, without his bothering his head about any forms whatsoever."

— from *The Seagull* by Anton Chekhov

One Hundred Miles
from
Manhattan

One Hundred Miles
from
Manhattan

A MODERN NOVEL
IN
TEN POINTS OF VIEW

CHRIS ORCUTT

One Hundred Miles from Manhattan

A Modern Novel in Ten Points of View

by
Chris Orcutt

Second Print Edition: 2015

ISBN-13: 978-0615999838 (Have Pen, Will Travel)

The cover artist for this book is Elisabeth Pinio, a graphic designer based in the Silicon Valley. The book formatter is EBook Converting|High Quality Ebook Conversion: ebookconverting.com.

The author has permission and/or Creative Commons rights to use the following photos from Flickr on the cover of this book: "Hunters Wellies CARNABY BOA…" and "Turquoise and Brass Earrings and Necklaces…" by Maegan Tintari; "DSC_1255" (the fox hunt) by Bethany; "Fall Foliage" by Kimberly Vardeman; "Rape Seed Field" by Les Haines; "Mansion on a Hill" by Lucas Wihlborg; "Just a Perfect Day" by Alison Christine. The photo "Wellington Sign" is by Karen Kruschka.

Also by Chris Orcutt:
A Real Piece of Work (Dakota Stevens Mystery #1)
The Rich Are Different (Dakota Stevens Mystery #2)
A Truth Stranger Than Fiction (Dakota Stevens Mystery #3)
The Man, The Myth, The Legend (A Collection of Short Stories)

www.orcutt.net

For Alexas:

My Véra, My Hadley, My Muse

1

MIGHTY HUNTRESS

Until that early June evening in bed beside her much older husband, Caprice Highgate had never heard the screams of terrified cows. In fact, before moving upstate from Manhattan to Wellington she hadn't heard so much as a *moo* out of one. Even after three years, on nights like this she longed for the white noise of the city. The sustained silence of the country was deafening, and when there *was* noise, like now with the wailing cows and the howling coyotes, it more than startled her—it shredded her nerves. She waved a hand at the open windows.

"I wish you'd do something about that."

Hamilton was reading an armchair safari book: Robert Ruark's *Use Enough Gun*. He turned a page. Caprice glanced at the double-barreled shotgun hanging over the bedroom door.

"Maybe try *using* a gun instead of reading about them," she said. "Did you hear me?"

"What?"

"Your cows. There are coyotes out there, Hamilton. Hear them?"

"Coyotes?"

"Well, they're not wolves."

"Stephen's on top of it, I'm sure," he said. "Take a pill."

"That's your answer—take a pill."

"Caprice, don't be melodramatic."

She put on her robe and went downstairs.

She poured herself a glass of wine, padded into the great room, opened the French doors and sat in an armchair facing outside. For a minute it was pin-quiet, but then another burst of the melee shattered the silence: the calves' bleats for help, followed by the coyotes' eerie whistles. She sipped some wine and gazed out into the darkness. Half a mile away, Celia's bedroom lights glared across the long, narrow pond (a moat, really) in front of the mansion. Caprice wondered how the first Mrs. Highgate was faring and whether the carnage was keeping her awake, too. She hoped so. She hoped the bitch died from sleep deprivation so she and Hamilton could move into the mansion. This place had always felt like a child's playhouse by comparison.

———◆◆◆———

In the morning after coffee, Caprice dressed in riding clothes and Wellies, got in her Range Rover and drove to the stables. One of the hands must have seen her coming because when Caprice got inside, Giorgio was already out of his stall with the saddle pad on his back. The air was thick with hay dust. She sneezed.

"Bless you," the stable hand said.

"Thanks. Stephen around?"

"Office, Miss Caprice."

She changed into her riding boots, grabbed her crop and helmet, and marched into the office. Stephen was on the phone. He raised a finger to her.

Caprice stood at the window and pretended to watch Giorgio being walked out to the yard. Instead, in the reflection she watched Stephen trace the curve of her backside. Caprice knew her ass was good, but the breeches helped.

"Miss Caprice," Stephen said, hanging up the phone. "What can I do you for?"

She fastened her helmet strap. "Have you *heard* the cows at night, Stephen?"

"Heard what?"

"You're as bad as Hamilton. Don't tell me you haven't noticed. The cows, the coyotes."

"Coyotes? *No*…they're not big enough to go after cattle."

She stared at him. "So you think I'm hearing things."

"No, it's just—"

"Saddle up, Stephen. We're going riding."

"Where?"

"Wherever the cows are."

He leaned back in his chair. "That won't be so easy, Miss Caprice."

Stephen launched into a monologue about Hamilton's 200 head of cattle being spread across all 2,500 acres of the estate. Since the animals wandered freely spring through fall, the noises Caprice heard—*if* she'd heard them—could have come from anywhere. As the estate manager, he knew about these things.

"Humor me then," she said.

"You're the boss." Stephen grabbed a rifle from behind his chair.

"What's that for?"

"In case you're right."

They rode all morning, scouring patchworks of fields separated by dense hedgerows. The weather was clear, affording a beautiful view of the Village of Wellington and the endlessly undulating, tree-dappled hills. They also saw a lot of Hamilton's cattle—Black Angus, Stephen informed her—as they searched for signs of the violence that had kept her awake last night.

As the noon fire horn carried faintly from the village, Stephen pulled up beneath the ancient oak that sheltered the Highgate family cemetery. The earliest stone dated back to 1711. Tiger lilies grew wild along the picket fence. Caprice loathed coming to this spot on the estate; headstones awaited Hamilton and Celia, but there was no space earmarked for her.

"Why are we stopping here?" she asked.

Stephen patted his horse's neck. "This is the last field the ruckus could've come from."

"What about Celia's side of the estate?"

"Sound wouldn't carry all that way."

"But we just heard the fire horn."

"Course we did. That's super loud."

"Wait a second." Caprice shifted in her saddle. "Isn't it possible you're simply inured to these noises—growing up in the country and all?"

"*Inured?*"

"Used to."

"Maybe. It's just…I've got a lot of work back at the office, you know? And don't you have that big party this weekend?"

She heaved out a "Yes," not because there was a lot left to do, but because Hamilton's turning 70 raised a recurring question for her: namely, what was she doing with a man over twice her age? Until recently, she had told herself the wealthy aged better than other people. But that was before he began to lose his hearing, a condition that dramatically highlighted the difference in their ages.

"We should probably get back, huh?" Stephen said.

Caprice nudged Giorgio into a trot and was practicing her post when Stephen called out behind her.

"I say, Miss Caprice…you've become one heck of an equestrienne. Yessir, you sure can sit a horse."

Of course she could. When a person had as much free time as she, with nothing to do but plan parties and serve on bullshit committees, and a modicum of self-discipline to take a riding lesson every other day, she damn well better be good at it. And then Caprice had a realization that made her feel hollow: *riding was the only thing that gave her life purpose.* How she had arrived at her current situation was suddenly a mystery to her. She was the second lady of the manor on Wellington's oldest and wealthiest estate. She had more money in her personal bank account than she'd made in a decade as a fashion writer. And she straddled her very own and very expensive thoroughbred. But she couldn't remember how any of this had come to be. It was as though she'd been in suspended animation for the past three years and had only now awakened.

"Goodbye, Stephen."

She trotted away. Then, flashing Giorgio the whip, she clutched his mane as he broke into a gallop, and together they jumped the fence at the end of the field.

———◆———

Mysteriously, for the next two nights there were no cow or coyote noises, and the silence made her wonder if she had imagined the whole thing. Mornings she half-heartedly combed a few fields, but finding nothing her interest waned. Afternoons were killed in the village: meeting with caterers, picking up Hamilton's birthday gift (a nude portrait of her by local artist Dwight Anderson), drinking organic Pinot Grigio with her fellow jaded trophy wives at the country club, and—her one respite—screwing local contractor Jimmy Tatko in his bachelor cabin on the shabby side of Chestnut Ridge. As usual, however, the sex did little to assuage the lack of purpose she felt.

The day of Hamilton's party, guests began trickling in at one o'clock for a soirée that didn't start until six. Some were friends who helicoptered up from Manhattan, but the majority were celebrities and nouveau riche with estates on neighboring hills—fellow hilltoppers, to use a local trope. And as if her hosting duties weren't stressful enough, in a moment of pity Caprice had agreed to share them with Celia. She then spent the entire party trying to avoid her.

When the well-wishers gathered around Hamilton for the cake-cutting, Caprice noticed that her husband, for the first time since she married him, was drunk. Sober,

Hamilton was a skilled raconteur; tonight, however, he was nothing but a malicious windbag.

"So Capreeez jumps out of bed and yells, 'The cows, Hamilton, the cows! There are wolves out there! Do something!' And I did do something…I read my book."

The crowd laughed. A woman Caprice didn't recognize clapped and said, "Oh, H.H.—you *scamp*."

To Caprice, it wasn't just that Hamilton was publicly making fun of her; it was his portraying her as a dumb blonde—which was incredibly hypocritical, since it was her hair and her intelligence that had attracted him in the first place. Standing behind his chair, she placed her hands on his shoulders and forced a smile.

"I said they *weren't* wolves, Hamilton."

"Oh? I could have sworn you said 'howling wolves.' But no matter. If I told you once, my dear, I told you a million times…you *must* stay away from the hallucinogens."

Celia was laughing now, in that closed-mouth sniggering way of hers—like a child trying not to. Caprice signaled to the band leader. The tent swelled with "Unforgettable," and couples drifted onto the dance floor. While Hamilton slumped in his chair and sipped Macallan 30-year, Caprice stole a cigarette from somebody's unguarded pack, walked outside barefoot across the cool grass and used the Rover's lighter. She strolled along the fence line in the darkness smoking the cigarette.

The moon glowed the fullest and brightest she'd seen since that summer night in Istanbul, during Fashion Week, when the moon rose the color of cantaloupe over a shimmering Bosporus, and was framed between two minarets of the Blue Mosque. Those were good times:

young and independent, partying and schmoozing all night, then rushing to meet her deadlines.

Now she stopped, leaned over the fence and took a squint-eyed drag on the cigarette. If she were still a fashion writer, how would she write about herself right now? Maybe, *"Caprice Highgate, of the Wellington, New York Highgates, went country-chic in a khaki linen sheath and raspberry toenails. And instead of jewelry—a simple gardenia in her hair. Stunning."*

She sniffed, shook her head, and squashed the cigarette out on the fence post. On her way back, something got her attention.

It was barely audible above the music, but it was there: howls, then long and plaintive moos. She cupped a hand to her ear.

It was coming from Celia's side of the estate.

She ran back to the Rover, drove to Stephen's office and grabbed his rifle. The only gun she'd ever fired was one at a carnival, but she'd seen enough action movies—point it and pull the trigger.

She went off-road between two fence lines and after a quarter mile reached an intersection. Caprice shut off the engine and listened again, then turned left and drove on until the moos and yips were nearby. When she reached the field the commotion seemed to be coming from, she opened the gate and drove in, killing the headlights as she climbed a steep hill. The tall grass brushed the side of the Rover and whispered in the wheel wells. *This is crazy, truly insane,* she told herself; yet the sensation of her pounding heart was invigorating. Her hands were clammy, her mouth was dry, but never before—never in her entire life—had she felt so sentient.

Near the top, the ground leveled. Dark shapes of retreating cows came into view. Hands tight on the wheel, she slalomed around them, then hit the lights. A dozen eyes reflected evilly back at her. She'd been right all along: they were coyotes, feeding on a calf.

She floored the truck, scattering them to the edges of the light. Two of them stayed put and shoved their snouts deeper into the calf's belly. She slammed on the brakes, jumped out with the rifle, and her toes sank into something warm and soft. She winced realizing what it was, but put it out of her mind and stamped around the vehicle.

The two remaining coyotes were burlier than the others. They turned, showed their fangs, growled.

Caprice watched herself in amazement: standing in the blue light of the headlamps, tucking in the shoulder-thingy, pulling the trigger. The first shot startled her, but it also got the coyotes' attention, and as they ran she followed them with the little bead and fired again. She fired three more times, each time thrilling at the gun's sharp *CR-AAACK!*, and when she looked up, she was alone beside the stinking calf carcass.

Still holding her finger against the trigger, without thinking Caprice let the barrel droop, and the gun went off. A burning sensation sparked in her calf, as though a hot curling iron were stuck to her skin. She raised her leg to the car headlight. Blood dribbled out of two small holes on the outside of her calf muscle.

She'd shot herself.

It was a sharp, blistering pain that at the same time felt strangely muted and distant. Maybe there were endorphins at work. It felt like last summer's hornet sting, and after the initial shock wore off, she became more concerned about two things. One, how a gunshot wound was going to affect the look of her legs, and two, how she could avoid getting blood in the Rover's interior. After wiping her manured foot on the grass, Caprice tore off the hem of her dress—a piece of trim she hated anyway—and cinched it tight around the wound. Then, glancing between the carcass and the Rover, she got an idea. She opened the tailgate and hauled out the tow chain.

The moon was higher now, illuminating the tire tracks she'd made driving in, and she followed them back to the tent with the calf carcass in tow. Guests, led by Hamilton and Celia, had gathered in the parking area. Caprice hobbled out of the car, reveling in the shock on their faces.

"We heard gunshots," Stephen said. "Your leg, Caprice! What happened?"

"No coyotes, huh?" She pointed at the calf carcass. "Who's hearing things *now*, Hamilton?"

———◆———

The following afternoon, as she sunned herself by the pool with her leg elevated, a young state trooper dropped by to take a statement about the gun accident. According to Dr. Hale, who had treated her immediately after the accident, her injury was minor compared to most involving guns, partly because it was such a small-caliber, high-velocity projectile (a .222 Hornet). The tiny bullet went through a small section of her calf muscle like a hot needle. Aside from the terrible itching, the worst pain was from the muzzle flash, which had burned her skin. The trooper took her statement, ogled her body up to her bikini top, and as he stood to leave, cautioned Caprice about using firearms.

"You really should leave it to the professionals, ma'am."

She opened her copy of *W* magazine and flipped a page. "Anything you say, officer."

That night, the carnage was louder than ever. It came from a field near the house, across the apple orchard. As Hamilton snored, Caprice limped out to the balcony and listened to the cries of mothers whose calves were under attack. In the case of the calf she'd found, the mother cow had been found stuck in a woodchuck hole with a broken leg. Stephen had had to put it down. Whether it was her own maternal instinct or a sense of female camaraderie that transcended species, before she knew it Caprice was clawing the balcony rail and wiping tears away with her nightgown. She had no idea why she felt this way—she'd never been emotional about animals—but one image kept recurring to her: the two dominant coyotes growling and showing their fangs. On one level she understood they were acting on instinct, yet there was something about their aggressive posturing that irked her. They were mocking her, like how Hamilton, Celia and their cronies tacitly mocked her. It was as though the coyotes were saying, "We'll do whatever we want, and there's not a damn thing you can do about it, girlie."

Oh, were they in for a surprise—all of them.

Worried that if she hesitated she'd change her mind, the next morning Caprice canceled all her riding lessons, withdrew from the upcoming horse trials, and joined the elite Chestnut Ridge Shooting Club and Game Preserve, cantering home at dusk with a sore right shoulder. When it came to motivation, it didn't hurt that her instructor was a quiet divorcée with gentle hands and gorgeous sandy hair. He also lavished her with compliments: that she had an instinctive feel for handling a gun, that she had two of the sharpest eyes he'd ever worked with, and that she looked great while shooting.

Each day, she shot skeet until lunch, then went to the rifle range and practiced on stationary and moving targets until dinner. She relished the new lingo: stock and breech, bolt and recoil, trigger guard and safety. She read articles about guns and shooting as she ate in the club dining room. The sole woman there every day, Caprice became a fixture, drawing groups of men who watched her shoot and admired her "form."

Oh, and did she mention the apparel? She loved her mesh shooting vest (peachy-pink and slim-fitting), and the rosy hue of the world through a sleek pair of Rydon shooting glasses. Strong yet feminine, the look suited her. Finally there was the weaponry.

When Caprice had been reporting on fabric and cut in the Michael Kors collection, she never could have imagined she'd one day have the same appreciation for gun craftsmanship—details like engraving, bluing and walnut burl. Allowing her instructor and the club armorer to advise her on gun purchases, she was thrilled to buy a Beretta SO-4 12-gauge shotgun (in a smart mahogany case) for skeet and trap. But for the coyotes she wanted something that, to borrow a sniper's expression she'd heard, could "reach out and touch" them.

"I'd suggest this one then," the armorer said. "It's a Kimber Longmaster VT, chambered in .22-250 Remington. Bolt-action, five-shot magazine. Detachable bipod for prone shooting. You'll want two scopes—a regular varmint scope and a night-vision one."

"Wonderful, I'll take it."

Caprice opened the bolt, held the empty chamber up to the light, and peeked into the gleaming barrel from the muzzle end.

She had never seen anything so clean.

She began to hunt. Every evening at sundown she drove to a field and waited for something to happen. A few times she heard noises in a neighboring field, sped over there and discovered that if there *had* been any coyotes, they were now long gone. She tried sitting outside in a folding chair with the gun on her lap, but the mosquitoes were too thick or she felt exposed. The coyotes, meanwhile, were killing a calf a week. Most of the time when she or Stephen found the carcass, it had barely been eaten, as if the coyotes were killing for sport, and once they'd terrorized a field, they didn't return. They were crafty, ghostlike creatures. To break the monotony of sitting alone in the Rover until two in the morning, Caprice invited her girlfriend, Jane, from hot yoga, who spent the entire time bitching about her 13-year-old daughter and questioning the morality of what Caprice was doing.

"I mean, they're all God's creatures, right?" She sipped coffee. "Who are we to kill them? They just want to eat."

"If you heard those mother cows crying, you'd understand," Caprice said.

Jane wasn't the only one; the entire village had grown distant and suspicious of her: the women she used to ride with, the ladies in the bank, even the kindly old butcher Mr. Bendini—even his nods and smiles were less frequent, more reserved.

She was in Bendini's Grocery one afternoon assembling a boxed supper for that night's hunt, when she spied Jimmy Tatko, sweaty from work, a T-shirt snug on his chest and shoulders, leaning over the refrigerated meat case. Jimmy waved a package of Italian sausage at her and raised an eyebrow. Caprice took a breath and shook her head no. He shrugged and swaggered to the checkout, slapping the Styrofoam package on his thigh, and for a moment Caprice stared lustily at his retreating ass and remarked to herself that the rhythmic slap of the package sounded a lot like when their two flesh collided.

"Caprice!"

It was a familiar woman's voice, behind her.

There was Celia, head to toe in tennis whites with a Birkin bag hooked faux-casually in the crook of her elbow.

"Caprice, we must talk."

Celia's housekeeper, pushing the shopping cart, walked away. Caprice closed her eyes and took a breath;

she would have preferred shooting herself in the *other* leg to talking to this woman right now.

"What do you want, Celia?"

"Not here." Celia straightened a pair of Dolce & Gabbana oversized sunglasses from three seasons ago. "My rose garden. One hour. It concerns *you*."

Too many times, Caprice had walked into an ambush on Celia's turf. This time, she decided, they would meet in the demilitarized zone.

"The waterfall," Caprice said.

Celia huffed. "Fine. But be prompt. I'm having guests."

When Caprice arrived, Celia was already in the middle of the rope footbridge, gazing at the waterfall and the exposed rocks below. She clutched the rope railing. A petite woman, Celia could easily be heaved over the side. The thought came and went.

"So," Caprice said. "Talk."

"Did you know this spot is the exact midpoint of the estate?"

"I did. Why do you think we're meeting here?"

Celia put a fist on her hip. The bridge wobbled.

"All right, do you know where Hamilton is today? No? With his *massage therapist*. Surprised? Oh, that's right, you've been shooting all day and so-called hunting all night." She paused for a moment and set her jaw. "Caprice, you need to resume your first job, which, as the trophy wife, is screwing my husband blind. I've seen this woman, honey, and you're good but not *this* good. She's an *Asian*, my dear, and Hamilton's always been a sucker for Asians. Oh, and she's younger than you."

Caprice crossed her arms. "Why are you telling me this?"

"Why? Because the devil I know—that's you, dear—is better than the one I don't. Honestly, Caprice, I loathe you, and I'm sure the feeling's mutual, but I don't want to go through another break-in period with a Caprice two-point-oh. Ours is not an ideal arrangement, but it works. I'm still Mrs. Highgate with the mansion, and you're Hamilton's younger plaything."

"Celia, what I'm doing isn't some *whim*." Caprice grabbed the rope railing. The bridge trembled. "Unlike you, I've had goals in my life and gone after them. There was a time when *I* chose the direction of my life."

"And right now you *choose* to hunt coyotes," Celia said. "Marvelous. Instead of playing your part of the trophy wife, you're going to throw it all away to shoot animals." She glanced at her watch. "I'll give you one last piece of advice. Whether you take it or not is your decision."

Caprice rolled her eyes. "Go ahead, get the last word."

"Since you insist on continuing with this *cause célèbre* of yours, do it right and be done with it. I know nothing about hunting, but it seems to me you're going about it poorly. Get a tutor, if there are such people, and finish this quickly. Every day you're playing the mighty huntress, the Asian gets closer to supplanting you."

Celia stomped off the bridge and disappeared into the trees. The bridge swayed. Caprice watched the waterfall. Oddly, about Hamilton's possible affair she felt nothing—not even a twinge of jealousy. What gnawed at her was Celia's insinuation that Caprice didn't know what she was doing.

It bothered her because the wily bitch was right.

———◆◆◆———

Evidence of Hamilton's new squeeze began to mount. Caprice didn't demean herself with laborious searches of his wardrobe or email; she simply kept her eyes open. In the pool house, for example, she happened upon a brochure for the woman's Connecticut day spa. But what unnerved Caprice the most—far more than having her territory invaded—was her own lack of emotion. Even when she found several long black hairs in Hamilton's Bentley, she was unfazed. Caprice began to realize she wasn't in love with Hamilton, and that, as nauseating as it was to contemplate, she had essentially been a high-priced, well-educated escort, and it would soon be time to move on. However, right now she couldn't think about that—about what leaving would mean to her sense of identity or future standard of living. Right now, her priority was eliminating the coyotes.

With a raving recommendation from her shooting instructor, Caprice enrolled in a two-week intensive course in big-game hunting at the elite MacLean Outdoorsman Academy in Montana's Bob Marshall Wilderness. Mitch MacLean himself was her personal guide. They rode horseback into the backcountry with a string of pack mules in tow. They camped and ate canned food, and she bathed in swift rivers as Mitch stood guard with a rifle. Besides coyotes, this wilderness was home to wolves and grizzlies.

She learned how to read tracks and spot game trails, work a hand-caller and use camouflage—especially on her face, which to coyotes was one giant white reflector. And because coyotes could smell humans for 300 yards or more, learning how to mask her scent was imperative. She told Mitch about the coyotes back in New York. Based on their pack-like behavior, Mitch said, they could be coy-dogs or even coy-wolves. Regardless, hunting them was an art, and when Mitch explained the advantages of tree stands, she contacted Stephen with specs and locations around the estate to build them before she returned.

Then, on the seventh day, Mitch told her she would be hunting that night.

"You're a great shot, Caprice, but this is the only way to know if you'll freeze up."

"I'm ready," she said. "And I won't freeze up."

Mitch took out the gun cleaning kit and set up a camp stool. Caprice saturated a cleaning pad with solvent and worked it with the rod through the rifle barrel. When she looked up, Mitch was smiling at her, shaking his head.

"What?" she said.

"My crappy luck, that's all. Let's see." He ticked off points with his fingers. "You're hot. You ride great—even if it *is* that English crap. And you're Annie Oakley with a gun. You don't mind roughing it, and you love it out here."

"What I've seen so far."

"*But* you're married, you live back East, and there's my luck for you."

"Well, things change," she said. "People change."

"Maybe." He straightened his hat and hiked up his jeans. "All right. When you're finished, take a nap. The first night is always the longest."

For that night's hunt, Mitch placed her alone on top of a bare hill that sloped gently south. With a clump of boulders for cover, the digital calling device upwind from her, and her face to the wind, Caprice was in a perfect position to take down any coyote that trotted across the field below her. Covering her rear was Mitch, who had set up downwind from her. He did it because coyotes were notorious for circling around and coming from behind to get a scent advantage.

And so there she sat, in the cool mountain air, in the darkness, listening to recorded shrieks of injured rabbits, waiting. Nothing happened that night. Or the next one, or the next one—each night with her sitting silent and painfully still for six hours at a stretch.

Then her final night arrived. The next day she would return to civilization, and the thought of not having taken a coyote was anathema to her. And it didn't happen until shortly after midnight.

The moon had floated over the trees, illuminating the field a shade lighter so Caprice could distinguish silhouettes. The shrieks of a wounded rabbit, disturbingly similar to a baby's cries, grated the still air. She scanned the horizon through the green glow of the night vision scope, and then, 200 yards away, the tall grass moved.

It materialized out of the grass, its pointed ears and pale chest coat instantly recognizable. It looked straight at her in the scope and sniffed. Caprice leveled the crosshairs on the animal's chest, exhaled and squeezed the trigger. Almost simultaneously with the crack of the rifle, the coyote fell over. Caprice stood up. Her leg was asleep as she ejected the spent shell and hobbled down the hill.

She had shot the coyote straight through its heart. Standing over the inert lump of fur, she felt queasy and lightheaded. After all, her quarrel was with the coyotes back in Wellington, not this poor thing. She was staring at the dead animal when Mitch walked up behind her and patted her shoulder.

"Don't worry," he said, "it didn't feel a thing."

When they emerged from the backcountry late the next morning, he drove her to the Missoula airport, and the two said goodbye—fittingly, she thought—in the shadow of a reared-up stuffed grizzly. Caprice was a mess. Her clothes were filthy and rank, her nails were ragged stumps, and her hair resembled the undergrowth she'd crawled through. And that wasn't the half of it. Her neck was covered with mosquito bites, her heels had blisters upon blisters, her teeth were scuzzy, her shoulders ached, and her nose, usually flawless, was peeling from sunburn. Mitch smiled at her.

"What?" she said.

"You look like shit."

"Please, don't sugarcoat it."

"But what I was going to say was, underneath you're still beautiful. It's like the patina—you know, on a bronze statue? It's a good thing you're leaving, actually."

"I'll admit," she said, "when those wolves got going the other night, your tent looked very appealing. And its occupant wasn't so bad either."

"Maybe another time."

She kissed him. He responded, clutching her shoulders.

"Goodbye, Mitch."

She picked up her gear, and as she walked away, he said, "Caprice?"

"Yes?"

"Be careful."

------◆------

At the foot of her interminable driveway, Caprice stopped to get the mail and newspaper from the box. She skimmed the headlines of the *Wellington Sentinel*: "Finishing School Fenced Off"; "Garbage Feud Leaves One Local Dead, Lands Another in Court"; and the one she was looking for—"Coyote Menace Escalates." From the poorly written article Caprice gleaned a few chilling facts. First, livestock besides Hamilton's had been killed in her absence. Second, a coyote approached a 3-year-old girl right in the village, and made off with the girl's toy rabbit. But the last item was shocking enough to make her unconsciously crumple the newspaper in her hands: Goliath, Hamilton's Jack Russell terrier, had gone missing and was presumed to have been killed by the coyotes.

Therefore it came as no surprise when she got home and found Hamilton slumped in a chaise precariously close to the pool, drinking Macallan straight from the bottle. He was positively incoherent. Exhausted from her trip, Caprice somehow marshaled the strength to help him upstairs to bed. There were long black hairs all over the pillows, and while piqued by Hamilton's lack of propriety, she was more angry at the coyotes for having put him in his blubbering state.

"Don't worry, Hamilton." She stroked his head. "I'll get them. I'll get them."

She found the Asian woman's phone number, called, and told her what happened.

"Get your ass over here," Caprice said. "This is the fun stuff."

She hung up, turned Hamilton on his side, brought him a glass of water, and went out again, taking her guns and camping gear. On her way to the fields, she stopped at the stable to see Stephen.

"Are the tree stands ready?" she asked.

"Yeah. Hey, you know the field next to Route 33?"

"Sure."

"Found a fresh deer roadkill outside there, so I dragged it into the field. The cows moved out, but that deer's nice and ripe. Should attract the coyotes."

"Good."

"Need any help tonight?"

"No."

She drove the Range Rover to a field next to the baited one, parked and hiked in with her gear, careful to hug the tree line and keep her profile low. In the tree stand, she applied face camouflage and bug spray, loaded the guns, readied the calling device, ate a Power Bar, took a No-Doz, checked the weather on her phone for wind direction (SSW at 4 mph), spread out her sleeping bag, and mentally prepared herself for a long and cramped wait.

———•◆•———

Her first sensation was pain. In her neck, her tailbone, her eyes. The rising sun pierced the trees and stabbed her as she tried to squint. She lay on something hard, but it was only once Caprice sat up that she realized she was still in the tree stand, 20 feet off the ground. A haze, not quite a fog, clung low and gray to the hillside, and like a veil blurred everything behind it.

Her head spun. Whether she'd dreamed it she couldn't be sure, but Caprice seemed to remember shooting all night long, as though fending off a siege. The coyotes came relentlessly to feed on the deer, which now, about 100 yards away through the haze, was an amorphous russet lump. There were other, darker objects scattered across the hillside, but at this distance, in the diffused light, they were impossible to distinguish. She grabbed her Beretta shotgun, checked to see it was loaded, and carried it down the rope ladder with the breech open. Once on the ground, she snapped the gun shut.

The grass was wet. She was glad she still wore her hunting boots. Which reminded her—*disgusting*—she couldn't remember the last time she had changed her socks. Hands tense on the gun, she crept across the field until she reached the deer carcass. The hindquarters had been decimated; many predators liked eating into a carcass from the rear because it was easier access. Blood spoor trailed into the gray haze. Caprice followed it, holding the shotgun at the ready because she couldn't see more than 50 feet ahead of her.

As she dipped into a hollow, she stumbled over a dead coyote. She'd hit it with a perfect kill shot. Fifty feet farther, she found another victim of her handiwork. However, rather than congratulating herself on her fine shooting, her "grace under pressure," or any of that macho nonsense, she was repulsed by what she had done. Originally she'd felt a protective impulse. Then, as the summer wore on, it was to see the thing through because nobody believed in her.

An urge to cry gathered inside her, but all she could do was let out a sigh and go get the Range Rover. She'd done enough. She'd proven her point—to everyone who had questioned her abilities and resolve, and, more importantly, to herself. It was time to let the authorities handle it.

She opened the gun breech and carried it with the stock on her shoulder. An accident now would be tragic. And speaking of tragic, thank God her former coworkers at the magazine couldn't see her—they'd faint. Then again, nobody thought "Trucker Chic" would catch on. Maybe she'd invented a hot new look: "Huntress Wild." Shambling through the grass, she played with the opening line of an article: *Ladies, if you want your wardrobe to deliver true shock and awe, get out of frou-frou boutiques, stop wandering sterile malls, and go where the guns are.*

Caprice smiled, took a deep breath and smelled something that, while not cow dung, was close—herself. When she got back to the house, Asian girlfriend or no, she was commandeering the master bathroom.

She neared the opening between the hedgerows to the next field. The early morning haze was thicker here, almost white, and so she heard but couldn't see something as it burst out of the undergrowth. It brushed her shoulder with its wings and darted low across the field behind her.

It was a pheasant.

Caprice relaxed and was passing through the hedgerow gap when a confused growl emanated from the haze somewhere ahead. She took a few steps back. Slowly the gun came off her shoulder and locked at the breech. The sound—part growl, part fearful whine—drew closer, and then a large coyote staggered into view. It stopped and swayed on its feet. If she hadn't known better, Caprice would have sworn the animal was drunk; but she had read about rabies in coyotes, and this one clearly was rabid and had to be put down. Her entire body shook with adrenaline, and she fought the impulse to run. She put the stock to her shoulder and took aim. The animal was stone-still, as though it had come to her to be put out of its misery.

She fired. The coyote collapsed.

Then, ahead in the haze was the sound of running. *A dog. Another coyote.* She hit the switch for the second shotgun barrel, dropped to one knee, and a large coyote ran toward her, growling savagely, foaming at the mouth. She waited until it was 50 feet away and coming head-on before pulling the trigger.

There was a hollow *click*.

All at once she felt her consciousness fly backwards across the field, away from the advancing coyote, yet her body refused to move. An instant later, realizing that the unthinkable really was happening, she got to her feet, flipped the gun over and held it like a club. The coyote accelerated toward the gap in the hedgerows.

Then it was blown off its feet and a blast rang out from Caprice's left.

A double-barreled shotgun, billowing smoke, edged into the frame of greenery.

"Caprice? Are you all right?"

It was Hamilton, followed by Stephen and a state trooper. Hamilton looked at the coyote he'd blown away. He raised the gun above his head and shook it.

"I'm impressed, Hamilton," she said. "And your timing couldn't have been better. My second shell was a dud."

"I'm glad you're okay."

The trooper stood up from examining the coyotes. "Rabid, looks like. I have to fine you, ma'am, for hunting without a license, but between you and me, I think you're gonna be a hero. Who knows how many of these things are running around the county? The state even."

"Good job, Miss Caprice," Stephen said.

"I just want a damn shower."

———— ◆◆◆ ————

Caprice had been debating whether to stay in Wellington, but when the following week the *Sentinel* ran a story entitled "Coyote Vigilante Cleans Up Wellington," she knew her days in this Upstate New York pastoral paradise were numbered. Small towns are ruthless in their judgments of a person, and once an image of somebody hardens, it becomes impossible to change it. As she entered Bendini's one morning, the entire store applauded. The men at the deli whistled more than usual when she walked by, calling in unison after her, "Hey, Caprice! 'Go ahead, make my day!'" And at The Country Fox, the hairdressers and clients chirped over Caprice's bravery and how they'd believed in her from the beginning.

But as much as she tried to resist it, day after day a single truth played in her head with increasing intensity: After the summer's adventure with the coyotes, there was no going back to being a trophy wife. She wanted bigger challenges and independence. She wanted to climb a mountain, run a marathon, scuba-dive with sharks. Travel to Antarctica. Go on safari. Help a family in need. Her adventure had left her brimming with confidence, confidence that she could do all of these things, or anything else that came her way.

And so it was that on a resplendent October morning, after having quietly dissolved her marriage to Hamilton with a fair settlement for herself, Caprice Oona Quinn packed her Range Rover with her clothes, saddles and guns, hitched up a trailer with Giorgio inside, and drove out of Wellington, leaving behind forever her years as a lady of the manor, toward an uncertain but exciting future.

2

HABITUAL THOUGHT

Carlton Hale, M.D., sat in an aisle seat at the Javits Center in Manhattan with his arms crossed. He was listening to a self-help guru.

"So remember," the guru said, "it is your *habitual* thought, not your periodical one, that decides your destiny."

The guru—Blaine Jameson, Ph.D.—strolled down the center aisle toward Hale with his palms pressed together—a caricature of spirituality. He stopped six feet away from Hale and looked around the packed hall.

"All right," he said. "So far this evening we've been talking about the keys to attracting abundance into your life. First, developing a crystal-clear vision of what you want. And second, staying with that vision with continuous faith and gratitude. Now I would like absolute silence while each of you closes your eyes and imagines what you want—in detail. *Live* in the house. *Drive* the car. *Hold* the money. And, most important, express gratitude for these things as if they're already here. So, go ahead. Close your eyes and start…*now*."

Hale clenched his eyes shut. After a few reluctant deep breaths, the first thing he imagined was taking the old woman sitting beside him up to see Jameson. She'd been to six of Jameson's lectures and was dying to meet him, so Hale was determined to help her. He had no doubts about her wish manifesting because he was resolved to plow through the crowd with her if necessary.

At this point the exercise became more difficult. Hale simply didn't know what he wanted. What else *could* he want? He was married to a bubbly first grade teacher, Emily, whose lilting voice reminded him of summer songbirds. She had a perpetually girlish face—perhaps because of her constant proximity to children—and a talent for gardening. Hale had a 6-year-old daughter, Molly, who looked like a miniature version of her mother, and who woke up every day with an infectious smile. He owned a rambling Victorian on a corner lot in the village, and the house, on paper at least, was worth twice what he owed on it. And he had a rock-solid practice as the only GP around Wellington who made house calls. The community had a seemingly inexhaustible supply of people 70–100 years old, and since most of them were absurdly wealthy, Hale charged a equally absurd premium for going to them—a premium that had paid for his Audi A8, his weekend getaway in the Catskills, and his membership at the Wellington Country Club.

Hale supposed he could visualize more of, or refinements of, the things he already had (for example, to shoot a 70 on the club course), but to do so seemed pointless. When you have everything a man could possibly want, there is nothing left to wish for.

Unable to come up with a new vision, Hale decided to think thoughts of gratitude for the profound abundance he already had. He cleared his mind, conjured up an image of his angelic wife, and ticked through a mental list of the things he loved about her. At item five or six—how no-nonsense she was about her hair—the image of Emily faded, and out of the darkness, as though entering from an unseen door far down a pitch-black hallway, a different vision appeared.

A woman.

A redhead.

A long-legged, C-breasted, flame-haired redhead.

The kind of redhead that could wreck a train.

She walked down to the footlights of his mind and smiled. She was in her mid-to-late 20s and for some reason had a Tiffany blue purse on her shoulder. Out of nowhere, a breeze came up and a wayward lock of her fiery hair scooted backwards across her pale, smooth cheek. Then the two of them were in a furniture store of all places, embracing and collapsing onto a deep green sectional. Her hair splayed across the fabric smelled of lavender, her breath, cinnamon, and Hale's hands were in awe of her body's surreal contradictions of frailty and fullness, of willowy limbs and sinuous curves. Her body arched eagerly to meet his touch.

He saw her in different outfits for a variety of activities, like a Barbie doll: Ski Resort Redhead, Symphony Redhead, Racetrack Redhead—every variation of her striking, and her hair—always her hair—fetchingly styled for each occasion: braids on the slopes in Vermont, an up-do at Lincoln Center, curls beneath broad-brimmed hats at Saratoga. She was forever smiling, and she loved to laugh. She was content to be his mistress. Yes, this was what he wanted: a gorgeous redheaded mistress, an utterly quaffable tall drink of water, delightedly insatiable in the sack. He fixed the image of her in his mind and meditated on it until Jameson resumed his lecture.

"Okay," he said, "now, letting go of what you want, I'd like you to open your eyes and share. But I don't want you to tell me what you want. Only how you *felt* during the exercise."

Although Hale didn't share, other audience members described feelings of bliss and satisfaction. "It's like what I want already exists," said a kiss-ass woman in the front row, "and I got to play with it in advance. Kind of like…a test-drive."

Appraising the crowd, Hale wondered how many of them wanted a better car, a nicer house, more money, or if any of them, like him, already had those things and instead wanted something else.

Something they weren't supposed to have.

Something dangerous.

At the intermission break, as the sycophants huddled around Jameson until only the top of his bald head was visible above the crowd, Hale guided the old woman to the front, through the throng of book-clutchers clamoring for the guru's autograph.

"Excuse me, folks," he said loudly, walking erect at his full six-foot-three. "This woman has been to half a dozen of these and wants to meet him. Let her through, folks, let her through."

When they reached the eye of the hurricane, Hale noted now warm and close the air was, clearly because of the overzealous mouth-breathers vying for the guru's attention. It was a slow-motion battle royal. Hale introduced the old woman and stood guard while Jameson posed for a photo with her and signed her three books. Jameson then placed a hand on Hale's shoulder.

His touch was warm and buoyant. Hale felt lighter, calmer.

"And what about you?" Jameson said. "What can I do for you?"

"Oh, nothing," Hale said. "I just came up to help her."

"Then *you* will get what you want," the guru said to his huddle of disciples. "This is the way of the universe. When we help others get what *they* want, the universe softens to us and brings us what *we* want."

As the crowd mumbled agreement with this, across the hall—far, far across the hall—Hale glimpsed a woman with flame-colored hair. Her hair was more than red, more than flame-colored; it was the color of Kilauean lava cooling on seaside obsidian. It was the fiercest, most brain stem-stirring red hair he'd ever seen. She wore a short skirt, and her long legs were crossed. Then, as if she had sensed his gaze, she turned and stared at him. After a moment, an anguished moment, an interminable moment that seemed to contain all his past defeats with beautiful women, her mouth burst into an enormous smile. Hale stopped breathing.

The crowd began returning to their seats, their heads blocking his view of her, so that when he made it into the open, he got turned around and couldn't remember where he'd seen her. He crossed the cavernous hall from the front, searching for that hair. He saw nothing but fading brunettes and dishwater blondes. Reaching one end of the hall and then the other without seeing her, he questioned whether he'd actually seen her at all.

For the rest of the seminar Hale stood in the back of the hall, sweeping his gaze across the sea of heads. He didn't see her. When it was over, he stood in the lobby and let the heads of hair pass by. Hers, unmistakable hers, wasn't among them. Half an hour later, the last person—a man yammering on a cell phone—trickled out of the hall. The Javits staff eyed him warily. He left shaking his head.

Outside the rain had stopped, but there was a raw April wind. He turned up the collar of his London Fog against it. Glancing at the line for taxicabs and not seeing the hair, Hale crossed Eleventh Avenue, heading east on 34th Street toward Madison Square Garden, where it would be easier this time of night to get a cab.

That hair, that hair. It was either a coincidence, which Jameson would say didn't exist, or Hale had imagined her. She had been too far away, and his view of her too brief, for him to thoroughly assess if she was real. It was just as well. If she turned out to be real, and not a figment of his imagination from the visualization exercise, she would surely disappoint.

Traffic was sparse and the street smelled pleasantly piquant, the way Manhattan does after a hard, cleansing rain. Light from a diner glared onto the sidewalk and made the pavement glitter. A couple of cars splashed through puddles. Hale was considering going in for a cup of coffee, a cinnamon roll and some *noir* atmosphere when a cab whisked by, heading down Ninth Avenue. He tried to hail it, and then, as though blown forward by a gust of wind, the cab surged through the yellow light. It sped to the end of the block and swerved to the corner, where *she* stepped off the curb and into the cab, that hair jouncing flirtatiously on her shoulders.

"Wait, wait!" he shouted. He waved his arms as though signaling a rescue plane.

Hale ran across 34th Street and down the sidewalk toward the cab. The brake lights glowed as he reached the middle of the block, and the length of the cab's hesitation convinced him that she had seen him and told the driver to wait. But then the brake lights went dark and the cab lurched from the curb, rocketing downtown, out of sight.

Hale, breathless, perspiring under his trenchcoat, stood in the gutter shaking his head. He waited for another cab.

Even though she had been heading downtown, Hale looked for her again in Grand Central. He stood under the clock at the information booth, desperately scanning the crowd while he waited for the 10:48 to Wellington. But as the minutes ticked by, and the time of his train's departure approached without any sign of her whatsoever—not *one* redhead to be seen—his looking became more halfhearted, and the potency of her spell waned. He bought himself two Heinekens trackside and boarded the coach, casting a surly look around before collapsing into a seat for the 118-minute milk train home.

Even if she <u>was</u> real, Hale thought, *she's gone now.*

<hr />

The next morning over Emily's homemade waffles, when she asked him what he'd learned at the seminar,

Hale pretended to be preoccupied with his *New York Times* and the second round results from the Masters. He kissed his wife and daughter, who would be driving to the Wellington Day School together, and left in such a fog of thoughts about the mysterious redhead that he remembered nothing of his drive to Mrs. Barnes's. He came to his senses in the middle of her breast exam.

Although cosmetically enhanced, hers were healthy, and Hale was certain that the 30-something, rich and widowed vixen *knew* they were healthy but used the medical checkup as a pretext for getting a man's validation of her sex appeal. Here, Hale had to tread carefully. He had to balance stroking the woman's ego—once telling her that her *glutei maximi* were "simply epic"—with making cold, clinical statements about not detecting any lumps. Mrs. Barnes expected Hale to examine her with a thoroughness and vigor that bordered on a full-body massage. Indeed he was examining her on a massage table outside her basement sauna and her skin was still very warm to the touch.

"Okay, Mrs. Barnes," he said. "I'd like you to stand up straight while I get behind you."

She sighed as if he were making her do something she didn't want to.

"Oh, all *right.*"

She hopped down from the table and dropped her kimono. As she turned away from him, she smirked and waggled her tush.

Hale stared at a treadmill across the room and held his breath. Mrs. Barnes was beyond sexy—she was heady with pheromones—and if given the slightest puff of encouragement would topple backwards with him onto the conveniently nearby sofa. Starting from her temples, Hale probed and massaged down her cheeks, neck, shoulders, breasts.

Upon reaching her armpits, she giggled, and Hale, close enough to her bare back that he could feel the heat radiating off her skin, suddenly thought of *her*, the red-head from last night, and imagined that she, not Mrs. Barnes, was in his hands, and his *corpus spongiosum* and *corpus cavernosum* engorged with blood and stiffened. Taking another deep breath at the nape of her neck, he noticed it was an aggressive perfume, and not the lavender he'd envisioned. This discrepancy was enough to jolt him back into reality, but not before Mrs. Barnes shuddered in his hands. She groped behind herself and tugged his hips into her backside.

"Mmm, did you feel that, doctor?"

"Feel what?"

"When you smelled my neck," she said. "I came a little." She held his hips in place. "Oh, my. Seems *somebody* didn't mind."

"I'm sorry. I mean, it wasn't my intention."

"Well, it *was* mine." She put her robe back on and patted him on the chest. "Nice work, doctor. It's about time you got into the spirit of things. I was beginning to wonder about you."

"Mrs. Barnes...Gillian...you know I think you're very attractive, but...what I mean to say is, it was purely an involuntary response. Please, I don't want to get a reputation among my other patients."

"Forget it. So you got a hard-on, so what? It's natural." She moistened a finger and guided some hair behind his ear. "Wouldn't I love to know what got into that head of yours."

<hr />

The next three days were filled with back-to-back commitments. There were more house calls—among them Carmel Cruickshank, wife of the country club pro and a mild hypochondriac who avoided all direct sunlight. There were office visits and patient charts. There was a Rotary luncheon at the country club grill. There was a town council meeting. A golf lesson. A dinner party at the Wechslers. And between exams, resolutions, swings and cocktails, his thoughts went habitually to the redhead.

He was constantly refining his vision of her, the details he invented startling in their specificity. She had a seductive laugh. Definitely. Her skin, he decided, was more translucent than white—a whispery pink that made her perpetually appear as if she had just stepped out of a hot bath. And at times she moved with the gangling impulsivity of a tomboy—say, skipping down the sidewalk or running up a set of stairs—oblivious to her hair and her womanly curves and their effect on men like him: to cause them to crash their cars, or trip and knock their front teeth out.

On the fourth afternoon, following a pro bono morning at the fire department's blood drive, he went to his office just outside of Wellington Village, in the hamlet of Rabbitsville. His assistant was out to lunch. There was a pink "While You Were Out" slip on his desk. An insurance company had called, this time questioning Hale's prescribing blood work for a patient. *Idiots.* He tossed the slip aside and turned to the mail, and right on top was a brochure that caught his eye.

Somehow Hale had gotten on the mailing list of the Café des Artistes—now "The Leopard at des Artistes"—on West 67th Street. It was a restaurant he'd enjoyed a few times during his residency at Columbia–Presbyterian and to which he once took some conservative Midwest colleagues, who, much more than the French cuisine, enjoyed Howard Chandler Christy's famous murals of wood nymphs. Apparently the menu was now Italian–Mediterranean. Hale was about to throw the brochure away when he flipped it over and there, smack in the center of the page, was a photo of his favorite mural in the restaurant. Entitled *The Swing Girl*, it pictured a redhead swinging rapturously on a vine. Hale stared at the brochure.

Of all the murals in the place, they had featured his favorite—the redhead—in the brochure. No longer was the brochure a piece of junk mail; it was a sign, he was certain of it, and it was telling him to go there for dinner tonight. That it made no logical sense whatsoever seemed to elevate the idea to a realm above logic, above cause and effect, and strengthen its case as a sign. Years earlier he would have dismissed the brochure photo as a coincidence, but that was before Jameson's audiobooks. Just that morning, while driving between appointments, he'd heard Jameson discuss this idea in *SUPERABUN-DANCE!*: "*There are no coincidences—no matter how crazy something seems. If you see a fish truck drive by and something tells you to call them, even if you don't need fish you had better call, because in one way or another, your destiny is tied to theirs.*"

She is supposed to be there, Hale thought. He picked up the phone, and without a scintilla of doubt in his mind, called to make a reservation.

———◆•◆•◆———

Driving out of town, Hale started to call Emily and tell her he wouldn't be home for dinner when he hung up and turned the car around. He would go to the Day School and tell her in person. This small act of courage cheered him, making what he had planned feel less sinister.

He hated lying to Emily. It bothered him more than being unfaithful to her with another woman. Extramarital sex was natural for males, whose genes wanted to get into as many desirable females as possible, but lying? No matter how you tried to rationalize it, lying was ugly.

Also ugly were the Victorian ruins of Wellington Finishing School, which he was passing for the third time today. Hale shook his head. The deteriorating campus had become nothing but a magnet for partying teenagers and urban spelunkers, and the town council had decided to finally put a stop to it. In preparation for future demolition, they would soon vote on a proposal to fence off the property.

Once again, as it had every day so far this month, it began to rain. Hale switched on the wipers.

But what made lying to Emily particularly uncomfortable was the fact that the woman was so selfless and understanding. He considered telling her that Jaclyn Urquhart was at her Sutton Place penthouse and had contracted the flu, but what if Emily ran into her later at

Bendini's? Such was the trouble with having a prominent practice in a community as small as Wellington.

Racking his brain for a credible idea, he settled on a story involving Dr. Jameson. Its greatest strengths were its difficulty of being proved false and how neatly it dovetailed with existing facts. By the time Hale had parked at the school and knocked on Emily's open classroom door, even *he* was convinced of its truth.

The kids were in the middle of their after-lunch nap, and Hale found himself distracted by one little girl—of course she had to be a redhead—whose sumptuous hair spilled over her desk in a silky, shimmering mass. Emily was in the doorway. She led him into the hall and stood at a diagonal to him, peeking in at the children every so often.

"My darling husband," she said, kissing him on the cheek. "What brings you by?"

"Remember Dr. Jameson, the man whose seminar I attended the other night?"

"Of course."

"Well, he called my office. Invited me to dinner in the city. Wants a professional testimonial, I think."

When Hale finished, her eyelid twitched. For a second she looked about to say something, until she reached up and wiped away an eyelash.

"How exciting," she said.

"How do you mean?"

"The testimonial. You'll be in his literature, Carlton. Maybe on his book jackets. It might even bring you patients."

"Maybe, but I don't need any more."

"When do you think you'll be home?"

"Late. Late, late. If it goes really long, I'll stay over someplace. I'd have you come with me—"

"No thanks," she said. "Not with twenty-five book reports to grade and cookies to bake for play concessions. But in case you do stay over, remember you have an eight o'clock tee-time tomorrow with Mr. Highgate." She kissed him and touched his nose, lowering her voice to a whisper. "That means take it easy on the strip clubs and all your *wild* behavior."

Hale swallowed a reply.

As she turned to go back in the classroom, her skirt with stripes of Easter colors whisked across his leg, and he glimpsed her white stockings underneath. Behind her, the door to a storage room was open. Hale had long nurtured a fantasy of taking Emily into a place like that, at a moment like this—during nap-time, with the drowsy hush of a light rain outside—closing and locking the door, sealing her mouth shut with his palm, and ravishing her, all while the children snoozed next door. Part of him wanted to be a cad, a rake, a scoundrel—a type of man he'd never allowed himself to be, forever concerned with his grades, his career, his reputation—and he felt a strange sense of betrayal toward Emily, as though she, his wife, were entitled to his first act of depravity. He reached for her as she crossed the classroom threshold, and instead of grabbing hold of her fawn-like arm, his fingers only grazed her feathery cashmere sweater.

Another time, perhaps.

———◆•◆•◆———

Even though the cost of parking in Manhattan had reached new levels of extortion, Hale didn't want tonight's excursion to be restricted by a train timetable. Besides, road trips like this one were precisely why he owned such an expensive, powerful car: to be able to cruise at high speeds down the narrow, serpentine Taconic Parkway; to be cushioned from the outside world by tangy leather and heavy doors; and to be able to listen to *SUPERABUNDANCE!* as he drove. His attention drifted between the CD and thoughts of the redhead. Indeed, Hale had never felt like this—so impatient to get there, as though he were being tugged by the navel.

"*Free will,*" Jameson said over the speakers, "*gives us all the ability to want and attract all manner of things, some of which may not be the best for us. The bottom line is, since you become what you think about, you need to be very careful about what you think.*"

But Hale had thought it through, and he wanted this. He wanted a stunning redheaded mistress. He'd met a beautiful Wellington redhead, Victoria Hart, when he treated her blue-haired daughter for mononucleosis, but she wasn't *the* redhead. Besides, Hale was so vehement about keeping the details of his private life a secret that he went so far as to buy all his liquor in Connecticut. But the Manhattan redhead was different, and he was certain he could keep her separate from his life in Wellington. He already balanced his practice, marriage, fatherhood, golf, and political office, and he knew for a fact that there were several men at the club and in local politics who had managed to keep their extramarital arrangements quiet. If they could do it, so could he.

"Visualize and act as if what you want is already here," Jameson said, and as Hale paid the toll at the Henry Hudson Bridge and roared out of the gate, breezing past the slower traffic and settling in at the front of the pack, he looked at the empty passenger seat, imagined her long diaphanous leg there, and reached out his hand to stroke it. Upon crossing onto the island of Manhattan, the attractive force between him and the elusive redhead had sextupled, and Hale knew with absolute certainty that she would be at the restaurant tonight.

Without requesting it, he was seated upstairs at a table with a direct view of *The Swing Girl*. For a cocktail he ordered a Manhattan—a Perfect—and when it came he sat back and studied the mural. It had been years since he'd seen it.

There she was, the ecstatic nude redhead, swinging by, her hair fanned out wildly and consuming the greenery around her like a firestorm. Then Hale noticed the blonde nymph pushing her on the swing. Her petite features and cherubic, sisterly smile reminded him of Emily. She appeared to be pushing the redhead out of the painting toward him.

Hale drained his drink and ordered another. He watched the door. Convinced that she would walk in at any moment, he put off ordering dinner until the waiter brought Perfect number two and scooped up the extra place setting. Hale ate his dinner grudgingly, recalling afterward only that it had contained a lot of roasted red peppers and shaved Parmesan. He spent most of the meal dividing his attention between *The Swing Girl*, the door, and the bar, where some attractive young women—but not the redhead—honed their vampish arts. The practiced way they cradled their Cosmopolitans and exposed their throats was annoyingly mesmerizing. After two hours of waiting, Hale paid the check and left.

Inebriated but not drunk, he strolled toward the parking garage in a misty rain. Fog had settled over the island, containing within it the rich smell of salt air. Damn that redhead! He'd been so certain she would be there. The fact that she hadn't, on a night like *this*, when the weather itself seemed to endorse his adulterous plans, struck him in his tipsy state as the most unfair thing that had ever happened to him—or could happen. He jammed his hands in his coat pockets and kept walking.

A block from the parking garage, he passed a bookstore with an obnoxious three-window display of *SUPERABUNDANCE!* books, CDs and DVDs. A large photo of Jameson hung from the ceiling. There he was, the smug, bald son of a bitch, projecting positive thoughts and selling suckers like Hale on the idea that you can attract the things you want. Hale gave the photo the finger and started to walk on when he saw a placard at the bottom of the window. The bold type got his attention:

Experience Dr. Jameson's
SUPERABUNDANCE!
All this week at the Javits Center!
This week <u>ONLY</u>!

It was another sign from the universe. It had to be. What were the chances of his seeing this particular display, on this night, especially when he'd never passed this bookstore before? No, this was telling him to go down to the Javits, and since this was the final night of the seminar, he had to do it *right now*. He ran to the corner to hail a cab.

———————◆◆◆———————

For a behemoth convention center in the middle of New York City, the Javits was surprisingly desolate as he approached it in the cab. The windshield wipers squeaked.

"Pretty quiet tonight," the cabbie said. "Usually is when there's not a big trade show going."

With a single bank of windows glowing, it looked like a giant suburban supermarket at midnight, lit noncommittally so you don't know if it's open or closed. Hale tipped the cabbie well for the fast ride downtown and sprang out onto the curb. Hopefully his intuition was about to pay off. But when the cab sputtered away, leaving behind wisps of exhaust that drifted into the fog, Hale began to doubt.

The first door he tried was locked. When he did make it inside the lobby, a group of security guards stopped chatting and turned to look at him.

"Help you, sir?" said one of the guards.

Hale approached them. "I'm looking for someone. Any chance I could pop inside to see if she's here?"

"Sorry, no can do," the guard said. "Seminar's already started. But if you want to wait until intermission…"

"Okay, I'll do that."

Hale sat on a bench and stared at the closed doors to the hall. He checked his email on his phone. He didn't have any. He watched the guards. They seemed to be talking about basketball; one of them mimed shooting baskets. After close to an hour of this, the doors opened and Hale hurried inside. He scoured the hall from one end to the other looking for her hair, but there was nothing even close. He marched out shaking his head, thanked the guards, and left.

Unsure what to do, Hale paced along the curb in front of the entrance. The fog seemed thicker now. It was eerily quiet, yet from somewhere on the avenue he could hear the rattle of soda cans in a shopping cart, and the voices of two men arguing. The sounds were so clear, it was as if the men were right next to him. It was a strange sensation because while he could hear them through the fog, he couldn't see them at all.

He began to hear an echo from his footsteps. He stopped, and the sound continued. It was the clip-clop of boots, at a slinky, self-assured rate. Hale reached up to straighten a tie that wasn't there. He fumbled with his hands and stuffed them in his coat. He had stopped six feet away from an overhead light that cast a bright amber beam down at the cement. Then a shape began to emerge out of the fog. The redhead stepped into the light.

Like Hale she wore a trenchcoat, except hers was open, revealing a Tiffany blue dress underneath. She had a matching bag on her arm. She was everything he'd imagined—even more so because she was real. She stood six feet away, the fabric of her dress swelling with each glorious act of respiration. She nodded in recognition and smiled at him with the same vivacity as she had across the seminar hall that night.

"Well…," she said. "It's nice to know I'm not crazy."

"Same here. I've been thinking about you. A lot. Ever since the visualization exercise, in fact."

"Really?" Her shoulders scrunched up.

"Really."

"I came here the night after, looking for you," she said. "I decided to give it one last try tonight."

He had no idea what he should say next. The situation felt precarious—that if he said the wrong thing now, then she and all of the future promises of her would vanish before his eyes.

And then he was saved. (Or was he?) As though part of the evening's predestined program, a cab pulled up beside them. Hale felt the misty rain cold on his face as he opened the cab door without a word and helped her in. At her lingering touch on his hand, his pulse quickened. He slid in beside her.

"Where to?" the cabbie asked.

Staring at her, drinking her in like he had *The Swing Girl* earlier, Hale found himself replying instinctively.

"The Waldorf."

At this her eyes sparkled. He lunged for her, slipping his hands beneath her coat to feel her curves and willowy limbs. She softened into him and the kiss.

Hale gasped at how every detail of her was exactly as he'd imagined. Her mouth tasted of cinnamon; her hair smelled of lavender. After a few blocks in the cab, or several trips of his hand between her cheek and calf, she pulled away enough to talk breathily out of the corner of her mouth.

"Promise me one thing," she said.

"Anything. What?"

"That you won't fall in love with me."

In the amber of each passing street light, her hair became suffused with a unique, indescribable shade of red. That he had this phenomenon to look forward to excited him almost as much as the prospect of soon holding her bare body against his own.

"Okay," he said.

He sealed the oral contract with another kiss, and from that point on, at each carnal milestone for the rest of the evening, Hale presaged how being with her would gradually destroy his life. Walking into the lobby with her, he knew that every one of his drives on the course tomorrow morning would be a slice. Buying her a drink at the bar, he saw himself looking Emily in the eyes a little less squarely from now on. Making out with her in the empty elevator, he saw himself resigning from the town council to have more free time to spend with her. Watching her undress and basking in her Tiffany blue lingerie, he saw himself in a motel, in the middle of sex with her, being ambushed by a powerful sense of *What the hell am I doing?"* and staggering to the door to get some air. And following her into the shower, he saw himself one summer afternoon, alone at a gas pump near the Taconic and staring down the road, a prosaic stretch of road that could lead him to her in two hours, and realizing that it was impossible for him to live a carefree existence anymore, knowing that *she* was out there.

Still, even seeing all of this in advance, when she opened the covers, snuggled down on the plush mattress, and squinted delightedly for him to clamber between her legs, he couldn't stop himself. It was too late. He considered the hundreds of times he had thought about her over the past few days, how often he would think about her in the future, and, as he marveled at the warm pink hue of her skin, Hale remembered Jameson's words:

"It is your habitual thought—not your periodical one—that decides your destiny."

3

RAIL TRAIL

When the conductor announced Wellington as the next and final stop, Victoria Hart went out to the train car vestibule and waited by the open door. A familiar pastoral movie flickered in the doorway—green hills and grazing horses, hedgerows and cornfields, woods and streams—but today she didn't bask in the images and reflect on how fortunate she was to live in the countryside. Today she was impatient to get the hell off the train and walk on the rail trail.

The train stopped and Victoria marched out the door, passing a younger woman who looked lost. The woman had a suitcase at her feet and stared at the road beyond the station entrance. A twinge of compassion, a thought that she should help this woman, came to Victoria's mind, but it was trampled by her own selfish desire to see *him* on the rail trail. She ignored the woman and put her bag in the car. She took her keys and water bottle and entered the rail trail walking briskly.

To keep Crystal from repeating the Hart women's pattern of teenage pregnancy and single motherhood, Victoria had modeled a love life the polar opposite of her mother's. Growing up in Birch Winds trailer park, Victoria never got used to her mother stumbling in late every Friday or Saturday night (sometimes both) with a different guy. The two of them would carom down the narrow hallway kissing and shedding clothes, slam the bedroom door, and giggle and moan and shake the trailer walls for an hour. After that, or for a while anyway, all was quiet. That is, until the shouting started. God, the hateful, graphic things they said to each other! Then, he—whoever *he* was that night—left with a bang, and her mother began her ritual: weeping for an hour, starting the vacuum, and blasting Billy Joel's "Big Shot" on the stereo as she cleaned. The one pleasant thing to come out of the weekly chaos? The two of them going to Dunkin' Donuts at sunrise for fresh lemon-filled.

Victoria wiped her eyes. She was determined to end this cycle. Determined to the point that instead of letting herself be picked up by men in bars, she walked a rail trail, alone, hoping to bump into a man she'd only said hello to a few times in passing.

When she came out of her reverie, the late afternoon sky had morphed into dusk, making the woods that bordered the path dark green and shadowy. The trail ahead was an empty, endless stripe of blacktop through a tunnel of trees. She heard rustling in the brush. A doe and her fawn crept onto the path. Victoria stopped. The fawn still had its spots, and its head barely reached its mama's belly. The doe sniffed and the fawn pranced into the trees opposite. A few seconds later, the doe came sharply to life and bounded into the trees.

"Quite a sight, isn't it?" said a voice behind her. "Makes you glad you live in the country."

Victoria spun around. It was him.

"Sorry," he said. "Didn't mean to startle you."

"Oh, that's all right. I didn't see you."

"I live right through there." He pointed at a ragged dirt path that led off the rail trail and faded into the woods.

"Convenient," she said.

"I guess. But to tell you the truth, I liked it better when it was an abandoned train line."

"Well, that's no fun," she said.

Victoria noticed herself flirting with him—standing taller, arching her back, exposing her long neck. He was taller and more broad-shouldered than she recalled. He was in his mid-40s and had a clean-cut head of jet black hair. Classically handsome. Honestly, he looked like he came from a different time—the early 1960s maybe.

"Anyway, we're losing light," he said. "Shall we walk?"

"Sure, I'd like that."

She grabbed hold of her hair and made a production of draping down her chest. The maneuver had the desired effect, which was to make him glance there and clear his throat in agitation. They started to walk. Victoria held out her hand.

"I'm Victoria, by the way."

They shook.

"Martin," he said. "I've seen you out here alone a few times. You married?"

"No, never," she said. "You?"

"No, I'm a widower." He nodded grimly. "Seven years now."

"Oh, I'm so sorry."

Victoria hated herself for it, but a voice inside her cheered at this news. *Seven years!* Long enough that if she and Martin got involved, it wouldn't be a rebound relationship for him.

"That's a long time to be alone," she said.

He shrugged. "That's life, right?"

They emerged from the canopy of trees into the middle of a vast meadow. The sun was dipping below the horizon. Bugs swirled in and out of the final shafts of sunlight, and the whistling trills of red-winged blackbirds rose out of the tall grass.

"Beautiful," she said.

He turned to her and studied her face. "Yes, it is."

She felt herself starting to fidget, wishing that he would kiss her, but at the same time hoping he didn't. It was too soon.

He nodded at the sunset. "We should probably get back."

They walked in silence into the tunnel of trees again. The crickets and other night noises enveloped them. Ordinarily, with the twilight shrouding everything around her, Victoria wouldn't be walking with a strange man, alone. But something about Martin's earnestness made her trust him. He had excellent posture, which seemed somehow to make him more trustworthy, and he kept a respectful distance between them. And although it would have been easy to do in the twilight, he didn't try to "accidentally" touch her butt or brush her boob. Rather, he strolled along, breaking the silence only to remark on the silence itself.

"Isn't this something? Can you imagine a hundred years ago, what it must have been like?"

"Quiet, I bet," she said. "But there's so much ambient noise today, I'm not sure we can ever know what true quiet is."

"In its day," he said wistfully, "this was a terrific little train line. Cornelius Vanderbilt owned it."

When they reached the benches at the end of the rail trail, Victoria worried that he'd want to ditch her. Instead, he smiled at her in the light of the street lamp.

"So, how about we do this again on Saturday?" he said. "Meet right here. What do you say?"

Victoria's eyes opened wide. "Uh…sure. How about four o'clock?"

"I have a client meeting at two, so that should give me enough time," he said. "All right, it's a date. Well, not a *date*-date. You know what I mean."

"Till Saturday."

He took her hand as though to shake it, and kissed it instead. The kiss sent a jolt up her arm and neck, and made her scalp shiver. By the time Victoria came back to her senses, Martin had walked away.

"G—goodbye!" she said.

"G'night."

She watched him fade into the parking lot, then headed for her own car, business as usual. If there was one thing Victoria Hart never did, it was celebrate the arrival of a new man too soon.

During coffee break the next morning, unlike the other girls, who crowded around a tray of H&H bagels like lionesses around a kill, Victoria abstained from the tempting carbs. She didn't want to be puffy for her date with Martin tomorrow afternoon. Rebecca, the pushy and petite bitch from HR—"the steam engine in Capris," as Victoria had secretly nicknamed her—marched over brandishing a scooped-out Everything bagel heaped with cream cheese.

"So, Vicki…no carbs for your big date tomorrow?"

"What? Who told—"

"Joanne. But never mind that. Let me ask you something. How do you know he's really a widower?

"He said he was," Victoria countered. "And he didn't have a ring." She stirred her coffee and placed the spoon in the sink. "Besides, why would a guy make up something like that?"

"Sympathy," Rebecca said.

"She's right," Onyx said, pouncing into the conversation. "Better check into this guy. The widower thing? Might be bullshit."

Victoria put a hand on her hip. "I don't care what you guys say. Some of us aren't so cynical. I've got a good feeling—no, a *great* feeling—about this guy."

Some of that great feeling wore off overnight, however, and when she sprang awake at seven o'clock the day of their date, it wasn't from excitement, but from angst. Angst and dread. *What if the girls were right about him?*

She took her time with the housework and grocery shopping, so it wasn't until noon that the reality of their looming date hit her, and that's when she noticed her hair. It was horrendous. She wrangled a one thirty appointment with April at The Country Fox and by three thirty was scrubbed, made-up and standing in front of her closet, asking herself philosophical questions about her clothing options: *If shorts, at what point does sexy become slutty? Do Spandex leggings say that I need help keeping my flesh sucked in?* And, *How tight can a T-shirt be before it says I have other things in mind besides walking?* Clothes and hangers piled up on the bed before she chose a simple, flattering pair of yoga pants and a polo shirt. She marginally approved of herself in the mirror and drove to the rail trail.

Sitting on a bench with a view of Bendini's across the road, Victoria saw her clever, blue-haired daughter inside at the register. Victoria sighed. Crystal *used to* have long, auburn-red hair like her own. Once, not too long ago, the two of them had ridden around the village on bicycles and received dozens of compliments about their hair from neighbors and total strangers.

Four o'clock came and went. Jimmy drove by in his pickup truck. He honked, held a hand out the window. Victoria glowered at him in reply. She'd recently learned that he was allowing Crystal to drink beer when she stayed with him on visitations, the idiot. When he had passed, Victoria noticed the boutique owner whose name she couldn't remember walking toward the rail trail entrance. The woman gave her a pitying look, a look obviously meant to announce her social and economic superiority.

Before Victoria could dwell on the look, however, a forest green Range Rover squealed into the parking lot. Martin hopped out. Victoria was about to leap off the bench when she stopped herself. She stood slowly.

Martin walked over in jeans, a dress shirt and tie. He smiled. Victoria forced herself to breathe.

"Hey there, sorry I'm late," he said. "Nervous client. Lot of hand-holding."

"I can imagine. How'd it go?"

Martin yanked off his tie and pocketed it, then unbuttoned his collar.

"Great. They approved the final designs. We break ground next week."

"Amazing! What is it, a house?"

"You really want to know?"

"Of course."

"It's a twenty-nine-room mansion on six hundred acres. Pool house, stable, the works. My design beat nine others."

"My God!" Without thinking she squeezed his hand.

"It's great to see you," he said.

"Me—I mean *you*, too."

He kissed her on the cheek and pointed at the sky behind her. Rearing up in the distance was a bank of clouds the same color as a bruise.

"We'd better go," he said. "It's north of us right now. If we walk fast, we should be able to go a mile or so and turn around before it makes its way down here."

"Sounds good. Let's go."

It surprised her how quickly they found their walking rhythm together. At five-feet-ten Victoria was considerably taller than most women, and she had long legs; Martin was an inch or two over six feet, but had shorter legs. In no time they were lockstep, stealing amused glances at each other.

"Freaky, right?" she said.

He shook his head.

"What?" she said.

"Oh, nothing. I was just thinking, 'Hmm...if we walk well together, I wonder what else we might do well together?'"

Victoria playfully slapped his arm.

They reached the broad meadow where the other evening they had heard the red-winged blackbirds. Today the meadow was deathly still. Martin and Victoria double-timed it up the rail trail, toward the black-purple horizon. A breeze, cool and sour, blew in her face, tossed her hair. The sky flashed in the distance like a flickering fluorescent bulb in a dark closet.

As they left the meadow behind and entered a new tunnel of trees, a rumble cascaded across the countryside, the sound plowing through her. She was glad to be out of that open field, but as they continued and the time between flashes and peals of thunder shortened, she began to question the wisdom of her walking companion.

"Martin, shouldn't we turn back?" she said. "We're headed straight into this."

"We won't make it back in time. At this point, it's about finding shelter."

"You know somebody who lives up here?"

"No, but the Finishing School is up here. It's just a little ways off the rail trail. We'll go in one of the buildings and get out of this."

Victoria squinted at him. "Hmm, it's almost like you planned this."

"Sure," he said, walking faster, "I've been waiting to get you out here during a thunderstorm. As you'll see, I put a mattress and blankets in the main building, along with a hurricane lamp and a bottle of Chianti. It's amazing how you're falling right into my plans."

She ribbed him, and precisely then—first in a hesitant trickle, then at a chaotic rate without a millisecond between drops—it began to rain. They ran, sticking to the side of the rail trail, where the canopy of trees gave them some protection against the storm. Victoria's polo shirt was instantly soaked. Her hair clung to her cheeks. When they emerged into the open again, Martin tugged her off the blacktop onto a set of train tracks that had not been converted to rail trail. Weeds sprouted between the railroad ties.

They ran up a long curve in the track, and when they came out of the curve a minute later, Martin led her down a dirt road that crossed the tracks. They passed an old phone booth, miraculously intact, and jogged toward the sprawling and dilapidated Victorian buildings. Most of the windows were broken, and the shutters dangled. Victoria had been here before, of course (what Wellington local hadn't?), but in the heavy rain the place looked the spookiest she'd ever seen it.

The two of them were within 50 feet of the buildings when a tall chain-link fence blocked their path. Martin attempted to climb it, slipped off, and kicked the fence so it clanged.

"Dammit! They must have just put this up."

Victoria looked around. *The phone booth.* She yanked on Martin's arm and took off. The wind shook the trees, the sky flashed, and not far away thunder ripped the sky like a giant bed sheet being torn. When they reached the phone booth, the two of them were panting hard. Rain streamed off the roof.

"Here?" he said. "Victoria, there's no way we'll both fit."

She pushed the door open and shoved him inside.

They were helped by the absence of a pay phone itself; where a phone usually went, there was just a tangle of wires. Victoria pushed Martin back as far as he could go, then stepped inside and slid the door closed behind her. Thunder vibrated the tiny shelter, and the rain drummed on the roof and slapped against the glass. The inside of the phone booth was warm and dry from sitting in the hot summer sun, and with the storm growling and slashing only inches away, it gave Victoria the satisfying sensation of having outsmarted Mother Nature. The dusty dry smell, however, combined with the sudden change from cool and wet to warm and dry, made her sneeze into her sleeve.

"Bless you," Martin said.

"Thanks."

The storm had darkened the sky considerably, but there was still enough light for her to make out what was happening less than a foot away. He slicked his hair back. His dress shirt was soaked with rain and clung to his shoulders, his arms, his chest. As for herself, the athletic bra she'd worn underneath her now-drenched polo shirt, while flattening out her boobs, did nothing to disguise the fact that she felt chilled. She rubbed her arms. Her teeth chattered.

"Cold?" he asked.

"Yes."

Up to now, Martin had been compacting himself against the "far" side of the booth while Victoria leaned against the door. But then they each took half a step forward, and embraced. Somehow, when their chests touched and their arms enveloped each other, it was as though wet flint and wet steel had been struck together, and their combined bodily warmth instantly dissipated the chill.

They stood in the sudden gloom listening to the rain raking the glass—at times against all sides of the little booth at once. The thunder crackled and the wind howled wetly in the door cracks. Afraid that Martin would become self-conscious and quit the embrace, she didn't move—not even a finger where it touched the small of his back.

The booth shook, the glass rattled, and their stiff, utilitarian embrace thawed into a protective hug. Raising her head, Victoria looked into his eyes, his gray, gray eyes, and rose on her tiptoes to meet his parting lips.

Martin lifted her off her feet. A warm glow radiated down her neck and spine. Every woman, and Victoria was no exception, loves to feel light and fragile in a man's arms. He held her up so her breasts compacted against his chest and their faces were level. It was a kiss that could have become much more, but there wasn't room for anything else.

The girls at the office saw the changes in her—the dreaminess in her step, the joyous daze in her eyes—and needled her constantly, but Victoria was too busy enjoying her time with Martin to care: Saturday trips down to Broadway to see a show, evenings at her place for dinner and a movie with Crystal, and one afternoon at the Chestnut Ridge Shooting Club to shoot sporting clays. There Victoria got a good look at Caprice Highgate, whose natural prowess with a gun was the talk of the club.

One steamy Saturday, Victoria packed a picnic and the two of them went to Lake Minnewaska in the Catskills. They'd been seeing each other for over a month. They swam in the vivid blue-green mineral water, sunned themselves on a diving platform offshore, ate in the shade of a pavilion, and swung in a hammock, kissing. Victoria felt more like 16 years old now than she had when she was actually sixteen, pregnant with Crystal.

They had fallen asleep in the swaying hammock with the piney breeze washing over them, when Martin sat bolt upright, rocking the hammock.

"Shoot, I've got to go. I'm late!"

"What?" One side of Victoria's face had been squashed into the netting. She fingered the pattern of indentations on her skin. "Late for what? A client meeting?"

"No. It's…it's a group I belong to. I have to go."

"All right," she said, "just give me a sec."

Without warning, he rolled out of the hammock, almost dumping her in the process. He hurriedly packed their bags and the cooler, and started the car. As soon as Victoria got in, before she even had a chance to fasten her seat belt, Martin tore out of the parking lot and swerved down the mountain switchbacks, blowing past an RV on a straightaway. The Range Rover engine growled like a cornered tiger.

"So," he said, "we had a good time today, huh?"

Gripping the steering wheel at 9 and 3 o'clock, he roared into a turn. She groped around and grabbed the handle over her door—the one that, until this moment, she had thought was for hanging clothes.

"Could you slow down a little, Martin? What's the big rush anyway?"

"Well…my meeting starts at seven, and I have to take you back to Wellington first."

"What kind of a meeting is it?" she asked.

He didn't answer.

"I could come with you," she said. "It would save you time. Not to your meeting, of course—I could drive around or go to a diner until it's over."

He grimaced. "No, I don't think so. I have no idea how long it'll run."

Victoria nodded, and they spent the rest of the ride—over an hour—in silence.

She had him drop her off on Main Street in the village, saying that she needed to get some vacuum cleaner bags at the hardware store. But the second he drove away, she ran to her car—parked in front of Brittany's Gourmet next door—and followed him. It wasn't as easy as she thought it would be. The gap between them kept increasing, and two cars got between them. Half an hour later, he crossed the Hudson, wended down a narrow road flanked by empty warehouses, and emerged at an old brick train station. He parked and ran inside.

Victoria parked up the street with a clear view of the station building and the creeping, glinting Hudson River behind. This was a public building, so it couldn't be what she'd initially feared—a motel rendezvous with another woman. Two dozen cars filled the parking lot. It had to be some kind of meeting.

Was it AA? Possibly. Anytime the two of them went out to eat, he never had so much as a sip of alcohol.

But weren't AA meetings held in churches?

She didn't want to leave her stakeout, but after an hour she needed to pee, so she went back up the hill to a fast food restaurant on the main drag. When she returned, the station parking lot was still full.

What was going on in there? A poker game? A historical society meeting? Ballroom dancing? What?

For two and a half hours, nothing happened.

Then, at a few minutes after ten o'clock, the station door opened and a large group of men filed outside.

Freemasons, maybe?

Victoria ducked until the cars had whisked by, and when they were all gone, she went down to the station for a look around. She tried to peek in the windows, but blinds blocked the view in all of them. A dim light shone through a small window beside the entrance. The window was above her head, and she had to pull herself up on the window ledge to peer inside. A man stared back at her. Startled, she slipped off, scraping her elbow against the brick. A surge of adrenaline went through her.

When she caught her breath, something told her to take another look. She pulled herself up again. The *man* was actually a mannequin dressed in a railroad uniform.

Victoria got down and walked around the building. She wanted to find a clue as to what Martin had been doing in there, but with the exception of a faded sign over the entrance that read, "H.V.M.R.A.," the outside of the building was bare.

———◆———

A Google search for "H.V.M.R.A." yielded nothing. There were a couple of websites for Hudson Valley something or other, but nothing that included the mysterious "M.R.A." suffix. She didn't tell the girls at the office about Martin's secret meeting; she didn't care to hear their paranoid speculations about his character and what was happening inside the old railroad station. She kept her doubts to herself, and Martin and she continued to see each other.

Then he invited her to his place. Despite the number of times they had passed his house on the rail trail, for some reason Martin never invited her inside. But tonight was the night. He lived on the wealthier side of town, off a densely wooded dirt road with an absentee movie star his only neighbor.

Victoria drove down a long stone driveway that wound through the woods and deposited her into a clearing, where his house burst into view. It was a contemporary design, built of redwood maybe, with a shallow-pitched roof and at least two sides that were largely glass. Parked next to Martin's Range Rover was a silver Mercedes SUV. A tween girl sat in the passenger seat, typing fast on a phone with her thumbs. Victoria shut off the engine and grabbed her overnight bag.

As soon as she shut the car door, she heard a woman shouting. It was coming from the house. The shouting was muffled, so Victoria couldn't tell what the woman was saying.

From somewhere inside came a loud crash of shattering glass, and not ten seconds later a blonde woman, maybe 40, a Coach handbag on her arm, slammed the heavy door and stomped down a curving set of granite steps toward the driveway. Pausing halfway down, she unsnapped the purse and plucked out an electronic cigarette. It emitted a whitish vapor as she puffed.

She exhaled, threw her head back, and muttered something at the clouds. When she started down the stairs again, they saw each other. The woman primped her hair with her cigarette hand, took a drag and marched down the remaining stairs with her chin high and firm. Victoria smiled.

"Hello. We haven't met. I'm Victoria."

The woman rested the fake cigarette on her hip and flicked her eyes across Victoria's face and body.

"Kate," she said.

Victoria glanced at her, then the house.

"You have no idea who I am, do you?" Kate said. A mosquito landed on her arm; she swatted it and flicked it away.

"No, I'm afraid I don't."

"Let me guess. He's still saying he's a widower."

Victoria felt walloped. "Excuse me?"

"Forget it."

Kate puffed on the cigarette and waved her hands in disgust. She wobbled across the driveway in a pair of open-toed Jimmy Choo pumps.

"Look, I don't have time to spell it out for you," she said.

Yanking her car door open, Kate started to get in, then stood back up and stared at Victoria long enough for it to be uncomfortable.

"Have you seen the basement yet?" she asked.

"No, this is—"

"Good, you're in for a treat. The second you see the basement"—she threw her hands up in a grand, expansive gesture, like an orchestra conductor—"*all* will become clear. He'll try to tell you I'm nuts, and maybe I am a little, but the story of every marriage has two sides, and I'm telling you—*look in the basement.*"

She stared pensively over Victoria's shoulder before shaking herself loose.

"Ugh, God," she muttered. "What a waste."

With that, she slid into the SUV. Victoria watched it back up and creep down the driveway until it faded into the trees. Flushed and shaken, Victoria took her time going up the stairs and stopped in front of the heavy door. It had a big brass knocker. Of course she would tell Martin that she'd spoken to Kate, and so the question was, would he come clean? As Victoria lifted the knocker, she realized that any future with this man would be determined by whatever happened in the next few minutes. She knocked, took a breath and opened the door a crack.

"Hello? Martin?"

"Yeah, in here, hon," he called out. "Cleaning up. Keep your shoes on. Glass. A *lot* of it."

Victoria walked toward his voice, through an airy foyer with marble floors, past a tall ficus tree beneath a skylight, until the walls disappeared and she was staring at a wall of glass with a view of the surrounding woods.

"Hey, hon." Martin was squatted beside a metal table frame with chairs around it. Green-tinted glass covered the floor. He swept mounds of it into a dustpan and dumped it in a kitchen garbage can. "Sorry about this. Let me get this cleaned up and—"

"Was that your *wife?*" Victoria asked.

"Who?"

"*Martin,* don't play games with me. The woman I just met outside. Kate."

His head slumped. "Yes. *Ex*-wife."

"You told me you were a widower. What was that for? Sympathy?"

"No. Because she's crazy."

"Who was that girl with her? Your daughter?"

"No," he said. "Autumn is the result of one of her mother's *many* flings." He swept more glass into the dustpan. "Kate's bipolar, you see. I pay child support for Autumn as if she were my child. The whole thing is…well, like this…"—he waved at the sprawl of glass yet to clean up—"…a damn mess." He dropped the hand broom and dustpan on the floor. "To hell with it. I'll get the rest later."

When Martin stood up, he was sweating. Victoria had never seen him in such a state; before this moment, he'd always been so composed. He wiped his brow on his shirtsleeve and kissed her.

"You look great, hon. Seriously, nice dress. I, on the other hand, am disgusting. Mind if I shower?"

"Of course not," she said.

"We'll talk more about this, I promise." He gestured at the living room. "So, what do you think of the place?"

"It's marvelous. So…palatial."

He frowned. "But not sterile, I hope. Not cold."

"No, definitely not."

"Good. Let me shower and I'll give you the grand tour. Pour yourself a drink, look around if you like."

He left. Victoria found the kitchen and poured herself a glass of Pouilly-Fuissé from an open bottle in the Sub Zero refrigerator. *Hmm, so apparently he did drink.* For some reason, her hands were shaking. The confrontation with Kate must have bothered her more than she thought. She gulped down the wine and refilled her glass.

In the living room she collapsed into an Eames chair and crossed her legs on the padded footrest. The view of the woods was wondrous, with hints of the Catskills peeking through breaks in the trees. All her life she'd never set foot in such a beautiful house, a house that so confidently declared its owner well-to-do. And unless she had grossly misinterpreted Martin's behavior toward her, he wanted a woman in his life with whom he could share this house.

She swallowed another mouthful of wine and closed her eyes. She let herself melt into the chair, the wine beginning to relax her, and imagined herself and Crystal living here. It was so peaceful. But remote. Crystal would need her own car. Maybe Jimmy could help with that. Then, as though waking her from a pleasant dream, Kate's warning resounded in her head:

"I'm telling you—*look in the basement.*"

She sat up in the chair.

Kate might be crazy, but she did make an awfully big deal out of the basement.

Victoria had to see it. Right now. Before Martin got out of the shower. She had no idea what could be down there to make Kate so insistent about it, but if it was anything creepy or disgusting, she wanted to know so she could leave—immediately. She put down her wine, got up and started opening doors.

It was the third door she tried—between the kitchen and the foyer. She flicked the light switches at the top of the stairs and started down.

A soft hiss and clacking sounds grew louder as she neared the bottom. The basement was ablaze with light, and as she stepped off the final stair onto bare concrete, Victoria couldn't believe what she was seeing. She closed and opened her eyes, and looked again.

It was a train set. And not just one of those oval ones you'd see around a Christmas tree. No, the entire basement was filled with tracks, trains, houses, bridges, stations, depots, cars, *papier-mâché* hills, and tiny plastic people. Locomotives criss-crossed the artificial landscape, circling lakes, racing into tunnels, passing atop and beneath each other on stacked trestles. Gaping at the incredible detail, Victoria found herself shaking her head.

She looked at the train set more closely. This half of the basement was a scale model of Wellington, and everything was there: the train station, Bendini's Grocery, the diner, the antiques dealers, everything—right down to Victoria's condo. The Finishing School campus—every single building—was there. Even the phone booth where she and Martin had taken shelter in the storm was there, meticulously recreated. The only thing not true to life was the rail trail itself, which on Martin's model didn't exist; instead, sitting idle on the tracks were a black steam engine, several Pullman cars, and a red caboose.

She'd seen a large train set once—in Manhattan somewhere, at Christmas—but that was a joke compared to this. This was astounding, inhumanly perfect, something that had taken years to build. A casual hobbyist could not pull this off. Maybe it was the wine combined with the surprise, but Victoria felt the strength draining out of her legs.

"Victoria? You down there?"

She heard the galumphing of loafers on the stairs, and then he was standing beside her. He put an arm around her waist.

"See you found it. Pretty awesome, huh?"

"It's a lovely train set," she said.

His grip on her waist slackened. "It's not a train set. It's a *layout*."

"Sorry," she said.

He grabbed a cap hanging on a hook near the stairs. With slow purposefulness, he put it on. It was an engineer's cap, blue with white stripes, and had a picture of a locomotive and the initials "H.V.M.R.A." on it.

"Hey," she said. "'H.V.M.R.A.'—what's that stand for?"

"Hudson Valley Model Railroaders Association. Why do you ask?"

"No reason, just curious."

Martin got down on all fours and disappeared under the tables. He emerged across the basement through a small hole.

"Hey, hon, watch that bridge over there." He pointed. A steam engine pulling boxcars stopped in front of a bridge. The bridge began to rotate. "Pretty cool, huh?"

"Very."

"Hey," he said, "I'm going to futz around for a few minutes. Why don't you head upstairs. I'll be…I'll be right up."

As Martin manipulated levers, dials and buttons, Victoria studied the enthralled expression on his face, and how he had ceased to notice she was there. Turning to the stairs, she clutched the railing and began to climb. It wasn't until she reached the top and the steel door clicked shut behind her that she covered her face and began to cry.

.

4

HUMMINGBIRD'S HEARTBEAT

From the moment Nero Palmer first saw the house, he wanted it. Although rakishly modern, the type designed by an architect's architect, it somehow blended into the landscape, as though it grew out of the gentle slope itself. A healthy pair of oaks anchored the front corners of the house, and the windows gazed down an unfurling lawn at the distant Catskills.

Nero sensed he would live here someday. He had no logical reason for believing this; it was something he just *knew*. But it was a premonition that left him uneasy, because for some reason it didn't include his wife.

Once a week he and Madison went to the house to admire it from the road. Late spring into the fall, they walked there or rode their bikes. In the winter or on rainy days they bundled into their aging Acura, drove around the countryside and parked in front of 59 Lookout Road. They sipped coffee and mused aloud about what the place was like inside. She described a palatial master bathroom with heated towel bars and an omnidirectional shower; he, a living room with a chalet fireplace. They talked and gestured at the house until a figure appeared behind the glass or a car crept by. Then, with a final glimpse and a leaden sigh, they went home: to their 100-year-old Victorian with an underwater mortgage.

But on pleasant days like this one in high summer, they rode their bikes up Lookout Road, basking in the shade of the old maples and in the sweet breezes tinged with freshly cut hay, until they pedaled up the final hill to the dusty blue mailbox for number 59. There they straddled their bikes breathlessly and shared their thoughts about the place.

"Look at how perfectly it sits on that little hill," he said. "And those oaks. They're huge."

"Does this mean we'll have to name the place 'Twin Oaks'? Like in *The Postman Always Rings Twice*?"

"That's perfect. 'Twin Oaks'—yeah, that's what we'll call it."

Madison tapped his arm. "Someone's at the window. We should go."

"Screw them," he said. "I'll leave when I'm ready." He closed his eyes and seared the picture in his mind. It was a comforting routine for him. "All right. *Now* we can go."

He switched into the bike's highest gear and pumped downhill. He glanced in his rear-view mirror. As usual Madison was moving at a geriatric's pace. She shrank in his mirror until she and her gleaming yellow Schwinn faded into the haze, and then he banked around a bend and she was gone.

At the bottom he passed a mysterious black driveway gate. Nero wondered who lived there. Around Wellington—an Upstate New York playground for rich Manhattanites and the horsey set—a driveway gate usually signaled nouveau-riche or celebrity residents; the old-money landed gentry didn't bother with such affectations.

Why was he constantly torturing himself by dreaming about homes he couldn't possibly afford? Sure, there was a time when they could have swung it, like back in 2000 when he was pulling down a quarter-mil at J.P. Morgan, and Madison's HGTV program, *Organized Home, Organized Life*, was riding high atop the wave of home improvement shows. They could have afforded their Classic Six on Riverside Drive with plenty left over for a mortgage on 59 Lookout. However after 9/11, Nero was laid off, along with thousands of others in financial services, and Madison's program was cancelled. They were forced to downsize and move out of Manhattan.

Nero reached the top of the hill and glanced in his mirror for Madison. She still wasn't there. He waited. At the nearby Chestnut Ridge Shooting Club, the skeet competition had started. The gunshots resounded through the still and muggy woods like heavy boards dropped from a height and slapping flat against other boards. After waiting for another minute or two, he turned around and coasted back down the hill.

Rounding the bend at the bottom, he saw her ahead in a turnout, straddling her bike and talking to the occupants of a new silver BMW 7 Series. Madison was giving them directions, no doubt; she radiated competence. Nero rode over.

A man and a woman were in the car, both wearing white terrycloth bathrobes with "Waldorf–Astoria" crests. The driver was a forgettable man in his late fifties, his closely cropped silver hair matching the car's exterior.

But the woman? Here was something else, and it took his breath away. Nero's first thought upon seeing her was, *"Fuhhhhhhhk."* Early 30s, coffee-black hair, and olive skin that seemed to smolder. She looked like she'd been reared on a Mediterranean island—Crete, Capri, Cyprus.

"We've never meant any harm," Madison said. "You have a beautiful house, that's all."

The woman turned away briefly, revealing to Nero her one physical flaw: a prominent nose. Roman, aquiline—whatever you called it—on her it was striking, sexy even, partly because of her high cheekbones, and partly because, by the imperious tilt of her chin, it was clear she considered it an asset, not a liability. Then she leaned across the seats toward the driver's window, and her bathrobe billowed, exposing a palpably smooth neck and décolletage. Nero's eyes dilated. The woman squinted at him and pinched the leaves of her robe shut.

"That's not the point," she said. "For like a *year*, you've been coming up to our house and staring at it. It's creepy. How would you like it if strangers parked outside *your* house and pointed at the windows?"

"Listen, we're sorry," Madison said.

"No, we're not," Nero said.

"Excuse me?" The woman shifted in her seat, accidentally opening the robe again. She yanked it closed.

"You heard me," he said. "That house is gorgeous and we enjoy looking at it. It's not illegal, so there's not a damn thing you can do about it."

"I'll tell you what we can do," the husband said. "We can call the state police. I happen to know the troop commander down there."

"Go ahead, call him. The most he can do is ask us not to do it anymore."

"Or we could get a restraining order," the woman said.

"Sure," Nero said, "waste your money. Good idea."

The woman was visibly upset. The huffing through her nose was audible, even several feet away over an idling car engine. Nero wondered if she was this spirited in bed. He smiled to himself imagining it.

"What the fuck are you smiling at?" she yelled. "Stop looking at our house! Leave us alone!"

Madison tugged on Nero's arm and wheeled her bike away from the car.

"Stay away from our house," the husband said, "or there will be consequences."

"Oh, how clever," Nero said. "A threat."

"A fact," the man said.

As the man turned the car around, the woman lit a cigarette and threw a crumpled Parliament box out the window at Nero. It bounced off his leg and landed in the dirt. She smiled at him, but before he could infer its meaning, she took a deep drag on the cigarette and blew the smoke at him as though trying to make him cough from ten feet away. "Wait," she said to her husband. The car stopped. She leaned out the window and jabbed at Madison with the cigarette.

"You're Madison Palmer, aren't you?"

"I am."

"I saw that show of yours a few times. It was pretty good."

"Thank you."

The BMW roared up the hill and was gone. A cicada buzzed to a crescendo and quieted again. They looked at each other.

"Can you believe that?" Madison said. "They weren't even dressed."

"Look," he said, "if they don't want people checking out their place, maybe it shouldn't be landscaped like an *Architectural Digest* centerfold. Or put a fence by the road, some bushes, something."

They pedaled side by side around the bend, passed the gated driveway and started up the hill. Madison was moving so slowly, her front wheel wobbled to keep balance.

"Maybe we did violate their privacy a little," she said. "But they still seem snotty. They don't deserve such a nice house."

At the top he and Madison pulled over and drank from their water bottles. It was only ten thirty, but it had to be in the 80s already, and the humidity was so high that, as he stared out across an overgrown apple orchard, Nero could make out a haze in the distance.

They were about to start pedaling again when he glanced over his shoulder. The BMW was a football field back, parked on the shoulder. Nero wrung his hands on the handlebar grips. *What the hell was wrong with these people?*

"What's the holdup?" Madison asked.

She had stopped in the blue shade of an abandoned red barn. Nero gestured at the car with his chin.

"Nothing. Just our new friends. Looks like they're trying to follow us home."

"What do we do?"

"We go home," he said. "We'll lose them in the village easily."

They continued for a couple of miles, biking toward the village with the BMW creeping behind from a distance. At the corner of Dark Hollow Lane, Nero saw that they were *still* following them, and got an idea. He turned down Dark Hollow.

"Where are we going?" Madison said.

"We're getting rid of these clowns."

"Come on, Nero, whatever you're thinking, *don't* do it. They're not worth it."

He checked his mirror. The BMW had made the turn then slowed to a crawl, as if the man was reluctant to take his luxury automobile down the rough dirt road. Nero and Madison crested a short hill and coasted down the other side. He lost sight of the car.

As soon as he had turned down the twisty lane, a lane hemmed in by steep and rocky hillocks, he felt himself in uncharted ethical territory. What he had in mind was wrong, but *something* had to be done. He was damned if these two were going to follow him home.

Ahead was a hill that had stuck in his memory since he saw it two years ago. A maze of boulders sat on top of the hill, beneath the trees. On one of the boulders, another rock, maybe two feet across, teetered above a blind turn in the road. There the road narrowed to one lane, hugged the hillside, then pitched sharply downhill and out of sight. It was a brigand's wet dream.

Nero pedaled madly around the base of the hill, dumped his bike in the bushes and scrabbled up the rocky slope.

"Up here," he called down to Madison. "Hurry!"

He smiled. The rock was round and weighed 300 pounds, he estimated, but with the right amount of force, it would topple over and roll down the hill. Indeed, it was so perfectly situated for this purpose, it was as though it had been placed here during the last Ice Age just for him. When Madison arrived a moment later, she grabbed his arm.

"Stop it, Nero! Stop this now!"

"Get over there and tell me when they're coming," he said. "Quick!"

"Are you crazy? We could go to jail for this."

"Fine, I'll do it myself."

Nero could barely make out the whisper of the BMW engine and the crunch of the tires in the distance. He positioned himself so he could see down the road. The car came around the turn at the base of the hill and started its climb. Nero dug his shoulder into the rock. Now, to get the timing right. Too soon and it would tumble in front of the car; too late and it would pass harmlessly behind. Staring through a gap in the greenery, he breathed deeply and waited.

The instant he saw a silver flash in his periphery, he thrust forward, shoving from his legs with all his strength. The rock tipped over the edge. Zigzagging at first, it bumped into a log, then straightened out and gained speed. Near the bottom it bounced off a tree root, launching headlong toward the BMW, now in the final feet of the turn. Nero winced, and for a split second he wished he could recall the rock. It was heading straight for the woman's window. If it stayed on its current course, it would gruesomely decapitate her. Disaster was imminent.

Then the car accelerated minutely and the rock dropped, striking the rear wheel where the rim and tire met. The tire exploded, and the rim wobbled out of sync with the flattened tire. Heads whipped around inside the car. The brake lights glowed as the car staggered around the turn and dipped out of sight.

"All right," he said to Madison. "Let's go. Quietly."

At the bottom they mounted their bicycles and pedaled back toward Lookout Road. Behind them, the woman's voice rose up shrilly from the forest. Nero couldn't make out the words, only the tone—angry and confused. Madison coasted up alongside him shaking her head.

"What?" he said.

"Nothing."

"No, you want to say something. So say it."

"All right." She thumbed over her shoulder. "*That* is going to catch up with you. I don't know how or when, but it will. That's some bad karma, my friend."

"I don't care. They needed to be taken down a notch. It was worth it."

She shrugged her shoulders and passed him, leaving in her wake a palpable sense that she was abandoning him to karma's whims.

———◆———

For the rest of the summer into the fall, Nero and Madison avoided 59 Lookout. Although they never discussed the incident, Nero knew that Madison was uncomfortable looking at the place after what he'd done to the couple's car. As for himself, Nero's impulsive behavior had weighed on him. A few times he considered going to their house, admitting his crime and offering to pay for the damages, but the bill could easily be thousands of dollars, and he and Madison didn't have that kind of disposable income anymore.

Fearing the karmic payback Madison had foreboded for him, he started assisting with her community volunteer work: selling raffle tickets, canvassing for signatures, enduring elderly bores. Since moving to Wellington, Madison had joined the Library Friends, the Highgate Building Restoration Board, and the Finishing School Redevelopment Advisory Committee. The Finishing School was slated for demolition in the winter, and every Saturday for the past year the committee had met to review proposals for redevelopment of the campus. Up to now, Nero had avoided attending any of the meetings, but when Madison asked him to attend one in early October, he relented and tagged along.

The parking lot was packed and every folding chair inside taken. Nero stood in the back of the hall sipping a cup of muddy coffee. After an introduction by the Wellington town supervisor, committee members took turns speaking from a podium as PowerPoint presentations appeared on a screen behind them. Most of the audience sat with their arms crossed.

Nero scanned faces in the crowd. There were several village business leaders in attendance, including Mr. Bendini, the bank president and the bookstore proprietor. Then two faces in the far corner got his attention. It was the couple from 59 Lookout. The husband pointed at Madison on the dais and whispered something to his wife.

Slipping on a pair of reading glasses, the husband read the agenda while the wife sat with her hands in her lap, her distinctive nose in profile, her chin elevated haughtily. With country casual clothes and makeup on, and that coffee-black hair cascading thick and lustrous over her shoulders—hair to make an Indian hair merchant weep—she was twice as gorgeous as she had been in the BMW that summer morning wearing only a bathrobe.

Normally Nero would have stuck around to hear Madison, but he didn't want the couple spotting him, too. They might create a scene. He was about to leave when the woman flipped her hair, turned, and saw him. She studied him, looking as if she would nudge her husband at any second. Yet she was perfectly still, and as they continued to stare at each other, a smile gathered at the corners of her mouth. He nodded at her and threw out his coffee. Then, grabbing a donut from the refreshments table, he slipped out the side door.

It was liberating to get outside in the fresh air, especially on a day like this, with the air cool and the sky a deep crystalline blue—the deepest blue he'd seen the sky since the morning of 9/11. Nero shook his head as if to physically prevent those memories and images from coalescing in his brain. He strolled halfway down the hill behind the building, through a blanket of fallen leaves, to a bench beneath a fiery orange maple. He sat down and ate his donut. A wooden swing attached to the tree swayed in an imperceptible breeze.

He hadn't expected to see that couple here. Since that summer morning he'd thought about their house only once or twice, but he'd thought about the woman a lot. He kept an eye out for her constantly: in Bendini's Grocery, the paper store, the post office, the diner, the hardware store, the train station. One night, she and her hotel robe assets appeared in his dreams. She was cooking him chocolate chip pancakes in her robe when her sleeve caught on fire. She embraced him and the two kissed even though they were burning alive. Nero screamed himself awake, and when Madison asked him what his nightmare was about, he said he couldn't remember. A few days later, he realized he was infatuated with this woman. And now she was here, at the Finishing School meeting, as though his fantasies had drawn her to him.

He finished the last of the donut and dusted his hands. It was a cider donut, his favorite, spicy with nutmeg and cinnamon sugar. He was about to go inside and grab two more when a woman's voice spoke up behind him.

"Good donut?"

It was her. She sauntered down the hill, kicking the leaves as she walked. Her hands were in the back pockets of her jeans, enviably cupping her ass. Nero wiped his mouth with the back of his hand.

"A great donut, as a matter of fact."

"Oooh, nice."

He thought she was referring to the donut until she took hold of the swing and pristinely wriggled her backside onto the seat. Satisfied, she grabbed the ropes, kicked, and began to swing.

"So, your wife's on the Finishing School committee," she said. "Interesting."

She swung higher, stretching out with her toes at the top of the arc, trying to touch another branch.

"Yeah," Nero said. "One of her *many* community projects."

"Well, I've got to give her credit." She dragged her feet in the leaves. The swing arc shortened. "I'm too selfish to get involved."

"Me, too," he said. "That, and this stuff bores the crap out of me."

She stopped swinging and sat watching him with narrowed eyes and her head slightly askance, as though she had just insulted him and was waiting for his reaction. She rose and walked over to the bench.

"Mind if I join you?" she asked.

As Nero slid over, he wondered if she and her husband knew that he had rolled the rock into their car. If so, she didn't show any signs of it.

"You know," he said, "we haven't been by your house since that time in the summer."

"Yes, that."

Here it comes, he thought. *They saw us, and now they're going to sue.*

She reached in her pocket, pulled out a box of Parliaments and a lighter, and lit one. Smoking with one hand, holding the lapels of her suede jacket closed with the other, she stared pensively down at the woods.

"Well, I've given it a lot of thought," she said. "We were pretty douchey about that. I mean, you were just admiring our house, right? It's not like you were peeping

Toms or something." She exhaled and glanced at him. "You weren't, were you?"

"Weren't what?" he said.

"Peeping Toms."

"No, I was only interested in the house." He studied her glistening lips, her sharp but delicate jawline. "But that was before I knew what was inside."

The look she gave him could be summed up in one word: *conspiratorial.* They lingered over each other, then she turned her attention to the tree line again. Her cigarette hand dangled from the side of the bench. She shook her head and smiled.

"What?" Nero said.

"Nothing. I was just thinking. When we were following you, the strangest thing happened—we got a blowout."

"What? A tire?"

"Bizarre, right?" She exhaled up and away from him, out of the corner of her mouth, and gave him that conspiratorial look again. "I'm Porchia, by the way. Porchia Taylor. Pronounced like the sports car, spelled like a porch."

"Nero Palmer."

"*Ouch.* As in 'Nero fiddled while Rome burned'?"

"Afraid so."

"Well, don't feel too bad," she said. "My middle name is 'Minerva.' Yeah, I don't know what my parents were thinking either."

Her handshake was firm. She locked eyes with him. It might have turned into a staring contest had she not suddenly been distracted by something.

"Whoa, what is *that*?"

Down the hill a crow skimmed the woods, its black figure in striking contrast to the brilliant foliage. Three other crows were in pursuit. When Nero looked again at the leader, it appeared to be carrying a long, pink string. But the bird's talons and beak were empty. Then he realized the pink string wasn't string at all; it was the crow's entrails. He shuddered. Porchia slid across the bench and grabbed his arm.

"Oh, that's awful," she said. "Are they trying to eat him?"

"I don't know. Maybe he broke the rules or something."

The crow and its pursuers disappeared over the ridge line, but Porchia remained close to him on the bench. So close, in fact, that with her suede jacket unbuttoned, he could feel the give of her breast against his arm as she breathed. The black sweater she wore was lusciously snug, more glazing her torso than covering it. She glanced behind them, then slid her hand up his shoulder to the nape of his neck. She twirled his hair in her fingers, the nails skating across his skin.

"Wonderful," she said. "I love how loose and wild it is. David keeps his so damn short."

It had been 15 years since he'd felt the lingering touch of another woman. A buzzing sensation trickled down his spine and pulsated through his limbs. As she played with his hair, her dusky eyes became alight with mischief. He jerked away.

"What is this?" he said. "A few months ago, you wanted to run me over."

She dropped her cigarette in the grass under the bench and ground it out with her boot heel.

"I told David to follow you that day. Yes, at first I was angry about you guys staring at my house, but then I saw how you looked at me and I wanted to find out where you lived. I was in my bathrobe, remember?"

A sudden breeze scattered the orange leaves at their feet. The wounded crow returned, gliding in from behind them. It had lost its pursuers, but its entrails were longer than ever, like ribbons on a kite. It landed on the tallest tree at the base of the hill and gaped at the shockingly bright foliage. Its beak was open.

Fingers tickled Nero's neck.

"Did you hear me?" she asked.

"Yes, I heard you—your robe. Yeah, I was looking. It was tough *not* to."

She wagged a finger at him. "I knew it. I knew you were bad. From the second you looked at me in the car, I knew it. One of us can always spot another. Right?"

The squint she gave him seemed to have a challenge attached. In one smooth and rapid motion he swaddled his hand in her heavy hair and hauled her opening mouth inexorably toward his. Their tongues touched. She gasped, like she'd burned herself. Her mouth was smoky, but he didn't care. As they kissed and his hands explored her torso under the coat, Nero fleetingly recalled some of the other women he could done this with over the years, and he was glad he had held out for someone spectacular like Porchia.

While their eyes were closed, something slapped against his face. It was a leaf. Wet from the previous night's rain, it clung to both of their cheeks exactly where their lips joined. Nero threw it to the ground and pulled away from her.

"I think something's telling us to stop."

"Come on," she said. "That was a coincidence."

"I don't want to piss off kar—"

"Look!"

She leapt from the bench and pointed at the crow. It keeled over and plummeted into the trees.

"My God!" She clutched his arm. "Have you ever seen anything like that?"

Now he hoped that the leaf and the crow *were* coincidences. But their occurring in such quick succession seemed to make it unlikely.

"Let's go have a look," she said.

"At a dead crow?"

"Why not? How often do you see something like this? It's like a meteor, a UFO." She tugged on his jacket. "Come on."

With a backward glance at the building doors, he jogged after her. They met at the woods.

"No, it's more to the right," he said. "Over there."

He used a stick to machete some raspberry branches, then stomped his way into the thicket until he had created a path.

"Give me your hand," he said.

She slapped it into his with a wink. Her fingers were warm and smooth.

"How chivalrous," she said. "And my, what big hands you have."

He yanked her into him. Grinning, she melted off his body and pulled him farther into the woods.

Once through the thicket, they saw the crow, lying in a wide pool of yellow leaves with its wings splayed. Porchia led them through the leaves until they stood over the unfortunate bird.

"Makes you think, doesn't it?" she said. "Here one minute, gone the next."

"Yeah."

She kicked dreamily through the leaves. The way her short suede jacket ended above her surreal posterior concentrated his mind like nothing else. As yellow leaves rained down around them, Porchia shed her jacket, draped it on the ground, and regarded him over her shoulder with hooded eyes. His pulse quickened. He became aware of his breath. His focus narrowed until there was only her. This was the first time since meeting his wife that he'd felt the ache of animal desire—a dreadful nausea, actually—and there was only one cure for it.

He strode toward her. She faced him. A glow, like the corona of an eclipse, formed around her silhouette, and in the spotlight of his stare her various fine features came into sharp relief: her eyes, her bright lips, her heavy hair, her breasts, and the space between her thighs. When his conscience tried to speak, Nero smothered it beneath a pillow.

"I want you, Porchia. Right now."

She clucked her tongue. "First our house, now *me?* Don't you know what the Bible says about coveting your neighbor's stuff?"

He grabbed her, half by her rib cage and half by her jarringly Junoesque breast. He studied her simpering lips, his own hovering inches away.

Alone and out of sight in the crisp autumnal woods, it felt like they were in a nature state. Monogamy, adultery, the sanctity of marriage—these ideas didn't apply here. He and Porchia were simply two creatures of mating age whose genes desired the other's. Therefore it was perfectly normal that they should be kissing, yanking each other's pants down, and wrestling each other to the ground. It was perfectly acceptable that he should be mounting her, locking eyes with her, thrusting into her—all while clutching her hair and leaves in his fists.

Whether it was sexual tension that caused it, or the danger that their spouses might somehow hear their muffled grunts above the stillness of the woods, they came in minutes, and, as improbable as it was, they came together. When the fog of endorphins began to clear out of his head and reason slowly returned, his first thought was an odd one.

"We have to check for ticks," he said.

They stood up unsteadily, shackled at the ankles as they were by their own jeans and underwear, and examined each other from crown to calf. Each tolerated the clinical inspection with a gossamer smile, but for Nero, compared to their brutish rutting in the leaves, it was uncomfortably intimate. He found a tick on her, encamped beneath her left breast.

"Hold it," he said. "Found one."

"Get it!"

Lifting her breast, he briefly savored its pillowy heaviness before flicking the tick away.

"There. The rest of you looks good."

"Only good?" she said.

"Very good."

After they had buttoned up, they brushed each other off.

"I'm going to want you again soon," he said, pulling her against him. "A-sap."

"A-sap? Stop, you're turning me on again." She pulled out her phone. "Give me your number. I'll text you."

They exchanged numbers.

"And FYI," she said, "during the week I'm all alone up here, bored out of my mind. All I do is go to yoga and play tennis."

They shared one more groping kiss, then she inspected his mouth and wiped away all traces of lipstick. Once through the raspberry thicket, they parted ways, their hands uncoupling as soon as they reached the grass. They walked up to the building separately, entering it at opposite ends, and until that moment Nero didn't grasp the import of what had just transpired.

But when she breezed through the door across the meeting hall and their eyes unwittingly met, his chest pounded, he couldn't breathe, and he knew he was in trouble. His only consolation was that, by the flicker of delight that appeared on and vanished from her face in a hummingbird's heartbeat, he knew she was equally caught.

5

STOLEN DOG

I left the zoo at the Wellington School relaxed, breathing deeply of the fresh air and brimming with good will for all humanity. Still in the zoo's afterglow, I decided to stroll up the shady path and through the quad—my first time since graduation 12 years ago. I hadn't been back because I'd disowned the place. But that's a whole other story.

Wellington is a private school. Lots of brick. Surrounded by woods, rolling hills and horse farms, the campus has the quintessential prep-school look—the kind that photographs well during peak foliage. Today the quad was sweltering. It was a Saturday afternoon in late August and it hadn't rained for two weeks. The usually lush carpet of grass was brown in spots that the sprinklers missed.

A young teenage girl, tan and skinny, typed on a phone as she passed. She was followed by an older man, her father I guessed, carrying a stack of brochures. A small beagle trotted behind them.

Anyway, they were at the far end of the quad, almost to the parking lot, when another beagle—this one older and larger—rounded some shrubbery beside the chapel. It was panting heavily and staggering. Its back legs or hips were clearly hurting. The dog stopped every few feet to rest. It stared at the man and the girl disappearing across the lawn.

"Excuse me," I said. "Excuse me!"

The man glanced over his shoulder.

"Is this your dog?" I asked.

"Yeah." He clapped. "Come on, Barney, come."

Barney took two dragging steps and stopped.

"Barney, come, *now!*"

"Sir, the dog's limping. He's exhausted. He wants to be carried."

The man was halfway to me now. He had the walk of a rich guy with too much time on his hands.

"Thanks for your assistance, but I'll take it from here."

It occurred to me that I'd seen him and his daughter in the parking lot earlier, getting out of a black Lexus with Jersey plates. He walked a few steps toward Barney, then stopped and snapped his fingers like a wheeler-dealer.

"Enough, Barney. Time to go."

"I'm telling you, he wants to be carried," I said. "He's probably dehydrated. Look at him."

"You need to mind your own business."

Averting his eyes, the man crossed the rest of the lawn, head back, walking slightly duck-footed on his heels, his posture betraying none of the annoyance I'd heard in his voice. When he was standing over Barney, he snapped his fingers again and pointed at the girl—a pink and brown blur across the quad.

"Barney. Now!"

Barney looked up at him and panted. He raised a paw.

"Dammit, Barney, move!"

He kicked the dog in the rump. Only about as hard as you'd kick a ball to a toddler, but it was enough to provoke a yelp from Barney, as if the man had struck an existing bruise.

The shock of it made my entire body recoil. What I did next, I did without a conscious thought whatsoever; I did it because of my love of animals. When the man stepped back to kick Barney again, I shoved him away.

"You are *not* kicking this dog."

"*You*, asshole, are about to find yourself arrested—for assault!"

He didn't try for the dog again. Spinning on his heels, he whipped a phone out and dialed.

"Give me the state police."

While the man smirked over his shoulder, I just stood there, legs trembling. Dread and confusion washed over me.

How could this be happening? I only came to see the zoo.

Looking down at Barney, who was smiling despite his obvious discomfort, I marveled at this perpetually forgiving creature, and an idea flashed into my head, an idea whose simplicity made it seem brilliant at the time.

While the man's back was to me, I scooped up Barney and ran.

The closest building was the chapel. The dog was heavier than I thought. About the size and weight of a small sandbag. Fortunately he didn't bark or squirm. As

I bounded up the chapel steps, he looked at me, ears flat, panting, curious. Inside it was dim and musty. I sneezed. There was yelling from the quad.

"Hey! Get back here, assh—" The rest was guillotined by the heavy door banging shut.

Barney's panting echoed in the empty chapel. I didn't know why I'd come in here; it wasn't as if they could give me sanctuary. Something told me that having come this far, I would have to go all the way, which meant escaping with the dog.

I ran down the aisle, habitually crossing myself even with the dog in my arms, went through a vestibule, and burst out of the back door toward the football field. I had parked in the lot behind the grandstand. The shortest route was a diagonal across the field.

A sprinkler hissed in the end zone. Dodging the spray, I skidded and fell to one knee in the wet grass. Barney was growing heavy and I was trying not to jostle him too much. Every time I glanced down at him, he was panting happily, as if content to be carried like a football so long as he was being carried *somewhere*. Checking over my shoulder and finding it clear, I hitched him up against my chest and broke out of the end zone, across the freshly painted yard lines, fantasizing about football glory days that had never happened: my bulleting the winning pass downfield; jogging sweaty and euphoric to the sidelines; showering and snapping towels; wolfing down pizza at Vinny's; and driving back to the dark and frosty field with my cheerleader girlfriend, and the two of us screwing beneath the stars. The truth was, though blessed with a great arm, I quit after two days of training camp—a fact that occurred to me now as I huffed onto the sidelines at the 40-yard line with a film of sweat beneath my clothes, carrying not a football but a stolen dog. I ran around the grandstand, jumped in the car, and sped away.

Petting Barney I drove around in a daze, thinking to myself, *"You've got the dog. Now what?"* I wondered how many kidnappers had similar regrets minutes after the deed was done. When I snapped out of it, maybe half an hour later, I was bumping along a dirt road north of the village. Instinctively I must have realized the state police would be roaring to the scene on Route 33. By the time I crept into the village, two hours after the dog-napping, it was five o'clock, and the dog still hadn't barked. It wouldn't surprise me if the owner had had the dog's vocal chords removed. Seemed about his style.

I snuck Barney into my condo in my gym bag, let him out in the kitchen and gave him a bowl of water. "Be back soon, boy," I said, and drove downtown to the diner.

Like all criminals, I was going nuts not knowing what the police knew, and in small towns like Wellington, the diner is information central. I parked in the lot next door, behind the building where a realtor had hanged himself and where the newspaper now was located. A high picket fence shielded the car from Main Street and the diner lot. That's when I noticed my shirt. It was covered in dog hair. I tried to brush it off, gave up and threw it in the car. Times like this, a man's glad he wears T-shirts.

As soon as I opened the front door of the diner, a wall of sound hit me: people talking, cell phones chiming, children screeching, plates clattering, the order bell ringing furiously. The place was insane. It always was on weekends in the summer; meanwhile, come February, when the waitstaff really needed the business, Wellington would be a ghost town. I stood at the entryway, looking for a place to sit.

My usual booths being occupied, I took a stool at the end of the counter with a view of a little girl and a smoky-eyed Latina sitting in the corner booth. The girl wore a checkered blue summer dress with a matching ribbon in her pale yellow hair. She looked like Alice from *Alice in Wonderland*. She was hunched over a coloring book. The woman across from her, darkly beautiful the way only some Latinas can be, held up a flash card with a picture of a cat on it.

"*¿Que es esto?*" she asked.

The girl looked up from her coloring. Size-wise she couldn't have been older than 4 or 5 years old, but the seriousness with which she studied the card suggested a girl twice her age. I predicted great things for her.

"Cat-oh," she said.

"No. *Gato.* Gah-toh."

"Gah-toh."

"*Muy bueno. Ahora, por favor.*" She flipped the next card. "*¿Que es esto?*"

It was a picture of a dog.

"*¡Perro!*"

"*Excelente. Perrrro,*" the woman trilled.

Perro. Yeah, a dog all right—like the one waiting at home. The one that hopefully wasn't barking. I wondered if the cosmos was trying to tell me something.

Lorelei came over and went through the motions of taking my order, even though we both knew it would be the homemade chicken pot pie and a Heineken.

Poor Lorelei. If she were a light bulb, she'd be a 150-watt 3-way. Her boyfriend? A 10-watt refrigerator bulb. She opened the beer and put it down in front of me with a glass.

"What happened to you?" she said.

"What do you mean?"

She shrugged. "You're all sweaty. And in your T-shirt."

The speed with which I conjured a story shocked even me. It was as if my subconscious spent all its free time manufacturing this crap.

"Took some clothes and a couple of old TVs to Goodwill," I said. "Caught my shirt on something going out the door. Ripped the whole side of it."

She winced. "Jeez, lucky you weren't cut. They should have given you a new one—a shirt. I mean a *used* new one. You were right there."

Lorelei's hair was in braids today. I couldn't put my finger on it, but there was something about pretty women in braids that totally revved my engine.

"Yeah, I don't think anybody saw it," I said. "Besides, I didn't want them thinking I was one of those 'I slipped on your ice' people expecting a payoff."

"Because there are so many of *them* around," she said.

"Just put my order in before I spank you."

Biting her lower lip, she rapped me on the knuckles with her order book and walked away. Was it my imagination or was she deliberately swaying her hips in that skirt more than usual to taunt me? I liked Lorelei, liked her wit, and liked even more the idea of wiping that teasing look off her face by bending her over this Formica counter after hours, using those braids as reins, and nailing her so hard that we embarrass the ketchups.

I poured the Heineken, drank half a glass and snorted to myself. Sex again? Really? My ability to entertain dirty thoughts during moments of crisis was astounding. Today it was tinkering with fantasies about Lorelei while a stolen dog sat in my kitchen; two weeks ago it was leering into a young mother's cleavage at the town pool while she panicked about her missing purse. My high school girl-friend—a Vassar girl—once called me *incorrigible*. After I learned what the word meant, I decided she was right.

I was sipping my beer when a hand touched my shoulder. "Hey, you!"

I jumped in my stool and turned around.

It was Crystal, Crystal with the blue hair. She and her hottie mother, Victoria, lived in the condo next door.

"Scaredy," she said. "Got a phone I can borrow? My battery died."

"Not on me," I said.

"Shit. Seriously?"

"Seriously." I fished in my pocket and came up with two quarters. "Here." I gestured at the phone booth in the vestibule outside the bathroom. "Use that."

She took the quarters with a huff, opened the door and slipped into the vestibule. Damn, she was turning into an attractive girl. Forget that her hair was the color of windshield washer fluid—she'd grow out of that. Her body, however...well, since I was thinking about dogs, it resembled a whippet's: tall and lean with firm, compact haunches that filled out a pair of khaki short-shorts. Her mom, though, with her womanly contours, was even better.

Lorelei brought my pot pie. I broke the crust to let out the steam and drenched it in pepper.

"Put some pepper on there, why don't you?" she said.

"Bite me."

"You wish." Leaning over the counter facing me, she bared her teeth, gleaming and surreally white, and clacked them a few times.

"Damn, nice choppers," I said. "Hot. First thing guys check out on a girl, too."

"You serious?"

I paused with a forkful of pot pie and gave her a look.

"Dick," she said. "Oh, check this out. Tommy called—his brother, works in the kitchen over at the Wellington School?"

"Yeah?"

"Said some guy over there stole another guy's dog. Can you *believe* it? Guy runs over, throws the owner on the ground, kicks him a few times and takes off with the dog."

She put her elbows on the counter and angled her lips toward my ears. She had that musky, talcumy scent of women's antiperspirant beginning to wear off.

"If somebody tried stealing Riley," she whispered, "I'd set the sonovabitch on *fire*."

"I bet you would." I ate some pot pie. Delicious, as usual. "So, who were these two?"

"Guy with the dog's from Jersey. Nobody else saw the other one."

"What's he driving? The dog thief. I'll stay on the lookout."

"I don't know."

Ricky, the diner's lone waiter, plowed through the kitchen doors.

"Coming through! Lorelei, you got a bunch of orders up." The bell rang three times in the kitchen. "Better hurry, Carl's getting pissed."

"Listen," Lorelei said to me, "I want to talk with you. Meet me for a drink later? I need your advice about something."

"If it's your love life, guess what? Not your friggen counselor."

"Ten o'clock? Please? That Mexican place off the Taconic."

"Montezuma? Maybe."

She smirked. "You'll be there."

"Maybe," I said again, a hair less certain this time.

As I was wolfing down the rest of my pot pie, a pair of state troopers walked into the diner and stood behind a group waiting for a booth. They were wearing their hats, something I'd only ever seen them do during traffic stops, and they were scanning the diner. I dropped some bills, casually made my way to the vestibule, and shut the door behind me. I went to the phone booth. Crystal saw me, raised a finger. I rapped on the glass. She glared at me.

"Jesus, hold on." Then, into the receiver: "No, not you. Forget it, gotta go. I'll text you."

She hung up and pushed on the door.

"Pull," I said.

She yanked it open and sidestepped out with her hands against her chest and her palms facing out.

"Eww, I *hate* those things. Took me like ten minutes to make one call. So stupid."

"Listen to me," I said. "Your mom's not home tonight, is she?"

"No. Went to Foxwoods with Gram, why?"

"I can't tell you about it here. Meet me at your condo in fifteen minutes."

She looked at me deadpan.

"Buy me some beer."

"What? You're a minor."

"Uh, *yeah*...a minor with a taste for Sam Adams Summer Ale," she said. "My dad lets me have it—ask him. Heck, in Europe, kids start drinking beer at like eleven. This country is so uptight, it's ridiculous. I want some. *Get* it for me."

I froze. I couldn't believe this was coming out of her mouth. The craving in her voice reminded me of alcoholics I'd known.

"*Please*...," she said.

"No." I headed for the back door. "Goodbye."

I had just put my hand on the doorknob when she spoke up loudly behind me: "I'll tell about the dog!" Her voice jumped an octave and reeked of desperation.

I turned around. "What dog?"

"The one at your place. The one that ran to the back door a little while ago when I knocked. The one you stole. *That* dog." She put her hands on her hips. "By the way, dude, what the fuck?"

I took a deep breath and glanced out at the dining area. The state troopers, burly SOBs, squeezed onto stools at the counter. I sighed.

"What kind of beer again?"

———— ·•◆•· ————

Back at Wellington Arms, I brought in the beer and phoned next door. The line picked up before it rang on my end. I almost didn't recognize the voice as Crystal's—it was that fast and breathless.

"Did you get it?"

Barney stood at my feet, looking around and panting.

"Yeah," I said.

"Come over, I'm thirsty. Use the patio door. And bring the dog."

The call ended. I stared at my phone. What was with teenage girls now? They seemed to be growing up, or at least becoming aware of their womanhood, a lot faster these days. Crystal displayed a self-assurance that you seldom used to see in women until their mid-20s.

Giving this girl alcohol opened me up to all kinds of trouble. But for the time being, the alternative—being arrested for assault and stealing a guy's dog—was a greater threat. So long as I kept her inside and quiet about it, I'd be okay.

I put Barney back in the gym bag, left a hole for him to poke his nose out, and went next door. The sliding glass door was open. Inside, I closed it behind me and pulled the curtains shut. Crystal was playing a car racing video game on a 50-inch HDTV. I unzipped the bag. Barney hopped out wagging his tail.

"That him?" Crystal pressed a button and the game exited to a menu screen. She tossed the controller on the coffee table, among Diet Coke cans, potato chip bags and women's magazines. "Oh, he's *cute*. What's his name?"

"Barney. But how'd you know it was a *he*?"

"Really? I need to explain it to you?" she said. "Beer me already."

"Beer you? *Fuck* you. You're what, sixteen?"

"Almost," she said. "Come on, I set up food for the dog and everything."

"You're only fifteen?"

"And *eleven months,* dammit!" She thrust herself off the couch with her legs, like a kung fu master, and clapped her hands. "Come on, Barney! Food, boy, food!"

When she came back, I had opened two beers. I put one in her outstretched hand, but didn't let go of it.

"You *cannot* tell your mother about this. *Ever*," I said. "I like your mom and don't want her pissed at me. When we're done, we put all the empties and bottle caps back in the carrier, and I take them next door. Got me?"

She leveled her eyes at mine. "Yes, *sir*. Got you."

I released my grip, thinking she'd immediately start chugging, but she took a measured, ladylike sip, like a brewer testing a batch. She smacked her lips and nodded at the bottle admiringly.

"Oh, Summer Ale and your refreshing hint of lem-on—I *love* you."

We sat on opposite ends of the couch facing each other. She reached out with her big toe and jabbed me in the thigh. Her toes were painted a blue that matched her hair.

"What were you doing over at the *school*, anyway?" she said. "You told me you disowned that place. Whatever that means."

"My niece is coming out for a visit on Monday. I was looking for stuff to do with her."

"Your sister and brother-in-law coming, too?"

"No, just my niece."

"How old is she?" Crystal asked.

"Four," I said.

She snickered. "*You're* going to take care of a four-year-old. By yourself. You."

"Sure, I'm taking the week off. Hey, it's only a week—until my sister flies out."

"'Only a week,' he says. Got a car seat?"

"She's coming with one. My niece."

"Well, you'll need some help." She took a swig of beer. "Yours truly doesn't go back to school for another two weeks. I have a lot of babysitting experience and my rates are reasonable."

"Lucky me."

She tilted her bottle in my direction. "Don't kid yourself. Child care's a bitch."

"All right, you're hired." I scratched at my bottle label.

"So," she said, "what's your next move?"

"Move?"

"With the dog. You *can't* keep him. You know that, right?"

I looked at Barney. He lay in the middle of the living room rug, panting, glancing between me and Crystal.

"I know that," I said.

"Dude, why'd you steal him? Kinda complicates shit for you, don'tcha think?"

"The owner. He was mistreating him. He kicked him for crissake."

Crystal was drinking when I said this. She coughed.

"In *front* of you?"

"Yup."

"Fucker. Okay, now I'm glad you did it." She got up, put her empty bottle in the cardboard carrier and opened another. Instead of death-gripping it the way most teenagers do—shocked they're even drinking one and determined not to have it taken away—she pinched it by the neck between two fingers, like a Texas barfly. Her nonchalance worried me.

Barney trotted over and sat at the foot of the couch near Crystal.

"Good boy!" She scratched behind his ears. "Barney have a good din-din? Yeah? Yeah?"

Barney wagged his tail.

"Hey, how do you have dog food?" I asked. "You never had a dog."

"No, but we dog-sit for the old ladies around here. Oh, let's shut up about dog food already." She put her beer down and sat up on the couch Indian-style. "Why aren't you with my mom?"

"Victoria? I don't know. She's older, isn't she?"

"She's like thirty-two. You're what, thirty?"

"Yeah."

"Yeah, you're *way* too young for her." She rolled her eyes. "Come on, don't you think she's hot?"

"Sure," I said. "But I get the sense she thinks I'm immature."

"You're right, she does. But she also thinks you're cute."

"Come on," I said.

"She peeks out of the blinds at you sometimes. Not creepy-like. She just likes watching you walk."

"But what about that architect she was seeing? Or is that over now?"

Crystal shrugged and drank some beer. I'd always thought her mother was a fox but hadn't asked her out because from our small interactions as next-door neighbors—chatting at the pool, saying hello at the Dumpster, shoveling out our cars in snowstorms—I sensed that she viewed me as irresponsible. A lightweight. A fair assumption on her part, given that I was currently sprawled on her living room couch, drinking beer with her underage daughter.

The thing is, I might have been 30 years old, but I didn't feel like an adult. Definitely not old enough or mature enough to be a teenage girl's stepfather. I didn't even know how to *iron*, for God's sake, plucking my dress shirts hot from the dryer instead of ironing them, and hanging them right away so they wouldn't wrinkle. Little things like that made me wonder if Crystal's mom and I could ever have a relationship. Maybe we could start with sex and see where it went. Crystal nudged me with her big toe again.

"Can I ask you something?" she said. "And if I ask, I want an honest answer."

"All right."

"Do you think I'm pretty?"

I didn't bother to look; I'd already given the idea of her attractiveness some thought.

"Honestly? If your hair weren't the color of a friggen Sno-Cone, I think you could be a model. You're tall, you have excellent bone structure. Work on your posture and let your hair go natural—what's the color underneath?"

"Red. Like my mom's."

I nodded. "Yeah, I could see you as a model."

She smiled at this, curling her legs beneath her and sitting up straight on the cushion as if she had already resolved to rectify her posture. Barney put his front paws on the cushion next to my leg and stared at me. His ears were flat. He looked sad. Crystal swung her beer in her fingers like a clock pendulum. She seemed way too comfortable with alcoholic beverages for a girl her age.

"Dude," she said, "Barney's like, 'Where's my family, mister? You kidnapped me. *Why* did you kidnap me, mister?'"

She laughed spastically, flopping around on the couch and slapping her thigh. When it trailed off, there were tears in her eyes.

"That beer," I said. "Finish it up."

"What?"

"You heard me." I stood. "That's your last one."

"No, it's not."

I put the dog back in the gym bag and zipped it up. It saddened me that he had become comfortable peering and sniffing out of a small hole, and it didn't help that I hadn't heard him bark—once. His life with the man from Jersey might not be ideal, but at least it was familiar to him. Better than staying with a bachelor who won't take you outside except in a gym bag. Maybe initially I had been right to rescue him, but by now I had to assume the man had learned his lesson. Crystal drained the rest of her beer. I held out my hand.

"I want another," she said.

"Too bad."

"Maybe I'll tell," she said.

"*Maybe*"—I snatched the bottle away and shoved it in the carrier—"I could give a shit what you do. Maybe if you say anything to your mother, I'll just deny it. Maybe I'm trying to be responsible." I stared at her. "Okay?"

Her eyes were wide. She nodded as if in a trance.

"Good. Now I want you to get on the phone—or text, whatever—and find out, but be discreet about it, find out where Barney's owner is. He must have stuck around. That guy wants to see me arrested. You do that and I'll be right back."

As Crystal grabbed her phone from the coffee table, I slipped out the patio door with the beer carrier. I put the unopened beers in the fridge, tossed the bottles and caps in the recycling bin, and grabbed my phone. Then I went back next door.

I hoisted up the bag containing Barney. He moved around inside. Crystal put down her phone.

"Well?" I said.

"You were right," she said. "Black Lexus, Jersey plates, staying at the inn. The one out by the Wellington School."

"Fox Hunt B&B?"

"Yeah, that one."

"All right," I said. "See you."

"Wait!" She put her chin flat on the armrest and blinked at me. "Can I come?"

"No. If I get stopped, I don't want you in the car. Then I'd really be screwed. Both of us."

"Makes sense." She picked up the video game controller. "So, what're you gonna do, *turn yourself in?*"

"Screw that. I'm dropping Barney on the stoop, pounding on the door and tearing ass out of there."

"A decent plan," she said. "Want a tip?"

On the TV, engines revved and a countdown clock beeped.

"Sure," I said.

"When you're like a hundred yards away, shut your headlights off."

She was staring at the game, tilting her hands with the controller. I shook my head.

"Rob houses much?" I said.

She wiggled her shoulders. "I'm still pissed at you for taking those beers."

"You got two more than you should have." I headed for the door with the game blasting behind me.

"Hey!" she shouted. "Drop by later, play with me? I'll be up late."

I checked my phone—it was 9:26—and thought about Lorelei at Montezuma.

"Yeah, maybe." Then, with a crisp, decisive nod, as if bracing myself for the sprint preceding a long jump, I hitched up the bag with the dog and opened the front door.

If I hurried, I could do it all. I might even have time to leave the prick a note.

6

STORMY WEATHER

On a blustery, rainswept morning in late October, the day after his divorce papers were signed, Holbrook Van Horn went into The Country Fox to get a haircut. He had just come from his former father-in-law's estate, where he had walked out with a check for two million dollars.

Although the divorce agreement was explicit on the matter—that the settlement was hush money—Hamilton Highgate was a discreet and honorable man, showing Holbrook respect by not discussing his daughter's disgusting, public cuckoldry. Instead the two toasted their mutual, newfound bachelorhood (Highgate's wife, Caprice, had recently divorced him) with Macallan 50-year. Holbrook could still taste the warm, smoky shadows of that incredible scotch as he walked into the salon. He hung up his raincoat, leaned his umbrella against the wall and smiled at April.

The lovely April Westerly. Seated at her station, legs crossed in a pair of dark jeans. She was sipping coffee and reading the Lincoln biography he'd given her. When she looked up and saw him, there was an expression of gratitude on her face, as if by merely showing up for his appointment he had somehow rescued her. It was a facial expression that in eleven years of marriage he had never seen on Peyton's face, but which he saw on April's every time he came in.

"I can always count on you, Professor. Right on time." She held up the book. "I'm *loving* this by the way. God, I knew Lincoln was poor—the log cabin and all that—but damn, he was *poor*. As I'm reading, I'm saying to myself, 'April, if this guy could be successful coming from that kind of poverty, you sure as heck should be able to get somewhere in life.'" She stood, placed a comb in the book and laid it on the front counter. "Coffee? Just made it."

"Is it flavored?" He took off his blazer, putting the check in his shirt pocket.

"No, it's not *flavored*. Not after you chewed me out last time about the hazelnut."

"I don't recall chewing you out."

"Well, you made it *very* clear that you don't like the flavored stuff."

She filled a mug and brought it to him. It was his Wellington School mug. "You left this here. Tsk-tsk, the absentminded professor."

Lord, did she smell good—warm and flowery, like the inside of a florist's hothouse. She stood close, her hair brushing the shoulders of a snug turtleneck sweater, ribbed and royal blue.

"Oh, hope you don't mind," she said, "but I brought Dylan with me today."

"Not at all. Where is he?"

"Right over there."

Dylan was standing up in a collapsible playpen next to the sinks. April lifted him out and held him on her hip with one arm. The boy wore miniature OshKosh overalls and a red flannel shirt.

"Wow, he's gotten big. And cute. Young man, you look like a little farmer."

"Say hello to Professor Van Horn, sweetie. Say, 'Hi, Professor.'"

"Please, April. I'm not really a professor. Besides, I think Holbrook would be easier."

Dylan smiled, put a hand over his eyes and squirmed against his mother. April put him back in the playpen and picked up her coffee again.

Motherhood had made her curves more distinct. Overall, she was more womanly-looking now than she'd been two years ago, when he first began coming here. Even from a distance, April's carriage conveyed a quiet strength—physical, mental and emotional. Holbrook felt himself calmer and more confident in her presence, which was strange since she was twenty years his junior.

She gave the boy a See 'N Say. Dylan pulled the handle and the toy said, *"This is a horse."* A long neigh came out.

"I had one of those when I was his age," Holbrook said. "But the animal sounds aren't entirely accurate."

"Oh?" She sipped some coffee and smirked at him. "Well, I guess we should take it away then."

"Take *what* away?"

"The toy. I mean, if it's not *accurate*." She started to lean into the playpen.

"No, don't!"

"Relax, Professor." She laughed and placed a hand on his arm.

Holbrook wondered if the delicacy of her touch was because of some affection she felt toward him, or if it was habitually tender from her cosmetology training. She kept the hand there, at the soft crook of his elbow, but he didn't detect anything sexual behind the contact; it felt like kindness, that was all.

By the time he noticed that she'd removed her hand, April was at the front of the salon looking out the big storefront windows. He went over. The adolescent red maples lining Main Street shook in the wind, their vibrant leaves stripping off and flying away in bunches. Some leaves slapped against the glass and clung there. The lights went out, then flickered back on, seemingly dimmer than before.

"Wow," she said. "Stormy weather, huh?"

Holbrook stood close enough to her that their shoulders grazed. Still perplexed about her touch earlier, he wanted to test her comfort level with having him close to her. She didn't move. In fact, her shoulder hovered millimeters away, pressing against his every so often, as if pulled there, or as if she were secretly testing his comfort level as well.

"Yeah," he said, "if it keeps blowing like this, the leaves will be gone by tomorrow."

"Oh, I hope not." She turned to him, cradling her mug in her hands. "I love the fall. I feel like I never got to see it—the foliage I mean."

"Me either." He sipped his coffee and nodded at the wild wet blowing outside. "This reminds me of a line I love: '...and the cold wind would strip the leaves from the trees in the Place Contrescarpe.'"

"What's that?" she asked.

"It's from *A Moveable Feast*. Ernest Hemingway. I teach it in my American Studies course."

"What's the movable feast?"

"Paris," he said.

Her eyebrows arched. "You've been there?"

"I have."

"Wow. It's good, I take it," she said. "The book."

"A wonderful memoir. Published posthumously."

"Didn't he...shoot himself or something?"

"He did," Holbrook said. "Ketchum, Idaho. 1961."

"I'll have to read it. Soon as I finish *that*." She glanced with a smile at the thick Lincoln biography resting on the counter.

"I have plenty of copies," he said. "I'll give you one."

"Great." She walked over to her station, put down her coffee, and adjusted her hair in the mirror. "So, ready for a wash? Not that there's any rush. All my appointments canceled this morning with the weather. All of them. You're it."

"I'll try not to disappoint," he said.

Before he knew it, he was in the chair at the sink with the oversized cape covering him. He tilted his head back until his neck rested in the sink hollow, closed his eyes and basked in her scent. April rinsed his hair, applied shampoo and worked his scalp. Her fingers were strong. The relaxation crept down his head, his neck, his shoulders, his back. He kept his eyes closed while she rinsed again, and when he finally opened them she was looking down at him with amusement.

"You looked like you were about to fall asleep."

"April, this is the most relaxed I've been in months," he said. "As of this morning, my divorce is final."

"Congratulations? I don't know—should I say that?"

"In this case, yes. Thank you."

She plopped a towel over his head and guided him to her station chair. When he was seated, she studied his hair in the mirror, deftly running her fingers through it like a sculptor about to mold clay.

"So, what are we doing today?"

"I defer to you," he said.

"You always say that."

"Because you're the expert. You know what looks best."

"Okay." April pushed up her sleeves and got a comb and scissors. She handled them with a smooth and easy touch that Holbrook imagined Annie Oakley might have employed with her guns. April had begun to snip when she made eye contact with him in the mirror.

"So, I don't know if you heard, but Brett and I—Brett and *me?*—anyway, we broke up."

"It's Brett and I, and I'm sorry about that," Holbrook said. "What happened?"

She heaved out a sigh that fluttered his damp hair.

"Nothing happened," she said. "That was the problem. Here he is, this guy with a degree from Rutgers—no slouch of a school, right?"

"It's a good school. What's his degree in?"

"Finance, I think."

"Well, for starters he needs to be down in Manhattan."

"I know, right?" she said. "God, what I could do with that degree. And he takes it for granted. Works over in that friggen hardware store"—she pointed with the scissors down the street—"for ten bucks an hour, and all he does is complain about it. Complains and comes up with schemes. All of these stupid businesses and inventions he's going to do."

"Like what?"

"Oh, gosh, lemme think." She stopped snipping and stared at the floor. "All right. First there was the ice cream shop idea, then the movie theater, then turning the run-down Highgate building into a conference center. Then he had this honestly ingenious idea for an invention—I forget exactly what it was, but it involved car seats—anyway, he had this great idea, and I told him to go talk to Mr. Highgate about it, or maybe somebody at the bank, but he never did. He's a dreamer and a schemer, and I'm through with him." She shook her head. "I should have seen it coming. As soon as I knew I was pregnant and he didn't offer to marry me, I should have dumped him right then."

"You're being too hard on yourself," he said. "You thought he'd change, try to improve himself."

"That's for sure. And damn, was I wrong."

When she stepped back to appraise her work so far, her face landed in the light. Holbrook saw that while attractive in a fresh-faced way, April was hardly a supermodel. The better part of her beauty came from her youth. Her skin was clear and smooth, her hair thick and straight, her teeth even and white. In that moment, in that light, April was the doppelgänger of the woman he'd forever pined for: April's mother, Lisa—when Lisa was her age.

But Lisa and Peyton were the past; April was the future. He only had to help her realize…

"You know what the trouble is, don't you?" Holbrook said.

"Trouble?"

"Brett's a damn kid, a man-child," he said. "They all are at that age. They have no ambition, they don't know anything. They're useless. You need a *man*, April."

She stared at him in the mirror, then looked away and nodded. He continued.

"You're too smart, and you have too much drive to be with a guy your own age. Nobody else is going to say it, but I will. If you wait for a worthwhile young man to come along, you're going to be an old lady in no time."

"You might be right."

Returning to his haircut, she squeezed a length of hair between her dexterous fingers, stretched it taut and flat, and snipped off the ends. Holbrook, notoriously clumsy with his hands, marveled at how easy she made it look.

"What?" she said.

"Nothing," he said. "I enjoy watching you do this. I enjoy watching anyone who is an expert at what she does. And when the expert is as lovely a person as you are… well, it's even better."

She paused. Her hands holding the comb and scissors fell to her sides.

"Why, thank you, Holbrook. That's one of the nicest things anyone has ever said to me."

He smiled. "You deserve it."

Once she had been snipping for a few minutes with the rain pattering in gusts against the windows, she glanced at him in the mirror and said, "Hey, can I ask you something?"

"Sure."

"It's personal. About your…ex-wife."

"That's fine. Go ahead."

"Well, that swingers club stuff. Is that for real, or is that a rumor?"

"No, it's true, unfortunately."

Using a detached tone that he reserved for discussing Robert Frost's poetry, Holbrook told her about the members all wearing necklaces with identical pendants on them: a tree with a dangling swing. He had found Peyton's on the rug one morning, and she dismissed it. But then he followed her to a motel north on the Taconic—The Red Pony—where she and a dozen other men and women paired off into rooms. He snapped photos of her and confronted Peyton with the evidence the next day.

"That's awful. You poor man." She put her free hand on his shoulder and rubbed it almost imperceptibly. "She didn't know what she had."

He turned around in the chair and took her hand. "Neither did Brett."

Holbrook could sense she was close, keenly close to seeing him in a romantic light, and although he had something in his shirt pocket that he knew would sway her, he wanted April to want him for himself alone, not for his ability to provide for her and Dylan. Her hand in his was limp now, but he kept holding it anyway.

"What I'm saying is," he said, "Brett didn't appreciate you. You need to be with someone who appreciates you, who sees your potential and wants to help you achieve it. Brett would never do that for you. But I *will*."

An irritated look came over her face as she stared back at him. "You're crazy. How could—"

The lights went out. After several seconds, it was clear they weren't coming back on, and April withdrew her hand.

"I don't know how I'm going to finish your hair," she said. "I can't do it in the dark like this."

"What about a flashlight?"

"Uh, *hello*? I can't hold it *and* cut your hair."

Holbrook stood up and removed the cape. "I'll go get candles. Or a couple of hurricane lamps."

"No, something that runs on batteries," she said. "I don't feel like burning down Colleen's shop."

"Okay." He put his blazer and raincoat on and grabbed his umbrella. "How bad do I look? The haircut. Bad, right?"

She faced him and brushed some hairs off his forehead.

"Not great, but I doubt anyone'll notice. Hurry back. So we can talk, okay?"

"Right back," he said.

Holbrook opened his umbrella as he stepped outside. The rain rattled the fabric. Steadying it against the wind, he glanced up and down Main Street at the sheets of rain swiping the empty street, the scarlet leaves swirling wildly in the wind. He crossed the street at a diagonal, jumping puddles and downed branches, and jogged up the sidewalk. All of the shop windows were dark. The traffic light was blinking red. He passed Brittany's Gourmet, where half a dozen patrons stood at the windows eating pastries and sipping from paper cups. They looked put-out by the storm. One man conspicuously checked a heavy Rolex on his wrist. Holbrook jogged on to the hardware store and went inside.

The bell on the door jingled as it shut behind him. He collapsed his umbrella. There was enough ambient light from the window to see that the front counter was unmanned.

"Hello? Brett? Anybody?"

There was no answer. A display of wind-up clocks ticked behind the counter. The wind pushed at the windows.

Holbrook walked toward the back room weaving through the aisles. The store was dark, and he accidentally bumped into a shelf and knocked several boxes of nails onto the floor. A box broke open, scattering nails everywhere. He kept going. At the doorway to the back room, he called again, and when no one answered, he went to the flashlights aisle. He found a battery-operated lantern, but in the dark he couldn't read the box to see how many batteries it required. He was headed to the register, where he could read the box in the window light, when the bell jingled on the front door.

"I'm in here," he said loudly, almost shouting. "Don't shoot me."

"Who's there?" It was Brett's voice.

"Holbrook Van Horn."

"Professor?"

"Yes. Coming out."

Brett was standing behind the counter. He held up a paper cup.

"Needed the old caffeine. Gotta have it." He took a sip. "So, thought you'd try looting the place, huh?"

"No, it's for the salon. April was in the middle of my haircut when the lights went out."

"She tell you what happened with us?"

Holbrook put the lantern box on the counter. "Only that you two broke up."

"No, no, no." He put down his cup and crossed his arms. "That makes it sound like it was mutual. No, she *dumped* me. It's such bullshit, man. I love my little boy. No way she's taking him away from me."

"I doubt that's her intention."

"That's where you're wrong, Professor. You don't know her. She can be a real vindictive bitch, trust me."

"Maybe, Brett. Listen, I have to get back so she can finish my haircut."

Brett leaned over the counter and studied Holbrook's hair in the dim light from the window.

"Yeah, you'd better. You look like a freak. Need batteries for this thing?"

"Yes. I couldn't read the box earlier."

"No prob." Brett spun the box around. "Eight D-cells. Be right back."

"Ten?" Holbrook said.

"Yup."

Brett disappeared into the dark store and came back a minute later with his hands full of plastic packages of batteries. He dumped them on the counter.

"All right, so who's paying for this? You or Colleen?"

"Me." Holbrook reached for his wallet. "But I only have credit cards."

"That's fine. I can swipe it now and run it later, when the power comes back."

Brett wrote out the purchase on an order slip, then swiped Holbrook's card under an old-fashioned credit card imprinter. Holbrook took his card back.

"Got a bag?"

Brett groaned. "Jeez, you're taking *everything* today, aren't you, Professor?"

He thought of April, waiting for him down the street.

"I suppose I am," he said.

Brett produced a plastic bag from beneath the counter, put the lantern and batteries in it, and handed it to Holbrook. Tucking it under his arm, Holbrook went to the door. He tried to time the opening of the door with the opening of his umbrella, but his hand slipped on the knob and the umbrella sprang open, blocking his way out.

"Uh oh," Brett said. "Shouldn't of opened that in here, Professor. Bad luck."

"That's crap, Brett," Holbrook said. "Goodbye."

Back outside, the rain had eased up, but the wind was every bit as strong. Main Street was a river of red—burgundy, ruby, scarlet—in both directions as far as he could see. Holbrook dashed down the sidewalk and crossed the street. As he went up the salon steps, although it had been only minutes since he'd left, he couldn't wait to see her again. It was as if his foray into the autumn storm had washed away all previous images of her so that he couldn't remember what she looked like, what her voice sounded like. Walking in the door, he was excited by the uncertainty.

"April?" he said.

"Yeah, back here."

"I got it," Holbrook said. "It's a lantern." He put it on the counter.

Out of the darkness, she approached him carrying Dylan on her hip. Except as she drew closer to the window it gradually became clear that it wasn't April he was seeing, but her mother, Lisa.

"Hello, Holbrook," she said.

The way Lisa had the little boy in her arms, held tightly against one breast, took Holbrook back to another gloomy day, long ago, when Lisa stood at her locker next to the glass passageway that led to the gym, cradling her books in her arms. The power had gone out that fall morning as well, and with early dismissal, upperclassmen who didn't want to take the bus home were bumming for rides. Lisa had smiled at him. If only she had said something, if only she had asked him for a ride. Holbrook would have driven her to Alaska if she wanted. But she didn't ask him, and the string of dates, and Prom, and perhaps marriage that might have ensued from that first ride home never happened.

"Holbrook? What is it?" Lisa, still holding Dylan, smiled at him with her head askance, as though he were privy to some scandalous secret.

"Nothing. A little déjà vu, that's all. What brings you here?"

"Martin sent everybody home. No power over there either. I think the whole village is out. What about you? What are *you* up to?"

"I was in the middle of a haircut."

"Well, I'll let you get back to it." She grabbed the door handle. "And you'd better give my daughter a great tip. April? We'll see you in a little while?"

"Yes, Mom." She ran over to Dylan, pulled his rain hood into place and kissed him. "Mmm-ah! See you soon, sweetie."

"Lisa, wait," Holbrook said. "Take my umbrella."

"You don't need it? Thank you. Sorry to hear about you and Peyton, by the way."

"Yeah. Well, take care."

Lisa left. Holbrook and April watched Lisa and Dylan drive up Main Street with a flurry of leaves chasing after them. Dangling at his side, his hand brushed hers. And for several seconds, several glorious seconds, they held each other's fingertips.

"So," he said, "you wanted us to talk."

"Yeah." She squeezed his hand and pulled away. "I guess I don't understand what you had in mind. I think I'm thinking one thing and you're thinking something else." She opened the lantern box and the batteries, and started inserting them. "Hope I'm doing this right. I can't see the little plus and minus signs."

Removing his raincoat, Holbrook suddenly became conscious of his half-cut hair matted to his skull. His neck was starting to itch. He looked at her across the room, intently sliding batteries into the lantern. He walked toward her. The lantern flashed on.

"Got it!"

With a smile, she stood it on the counter. Holbrook shut it off.

"Hey," she said.

"What I have to say is serious." He took her hands. "As Dean of the Wellington School, one of the benefits I get is tuition at any school, for anyone in my family."

"Okay…"

"So, my son could go to the Wellington School, and my wife could go to college—anywhere she gets accepted. And there are some excellent colleges around here."

"Your *wife*, huh?"

"That's right."

"You hardly know me," she said. "Wouldn't it be like those Green Card people? You know, the ones that marry U.S. citizens to stay in the country? Seems like kind of a scam."

"Not if we cared for each other."

Holbrook switched on the lantern. He put a hand behind her back and awkwardly kissed her. When he finished, he saw in her eyes that while she had found the kiss pleasant, it hadn't convinced her. He was about to launch into a fresh argument as to why they were perfect for each other despite the chasm of age between them, when she glanced at his shirt.

"What's that?" she asked.

It was the check from Mr. Highgate, sticking out of his shirt pocket.

"Oh, that? Take a look."

Holbrook let go of her and stepped back so he could have a clear view of her face in the lantern light. As she unfolded and examined the check, her expression morphed before his eyes—from curiosity to confusion to mouth-gaping, breathless shock. When she looked up at him, that expression of gratitude, of being rescued, was there again.

But this time, it was more than that. Her face seemed to be glowing with something.

It was hope.

7

ARRESTINGLY BLUE

The first heavy snow of the season blanketed the Wellington countryside a few days before Christmas. I was cross-country skiing, or trying to anyway. Breaking trail in the deep powder was slow going. I'd been at it for almost two hours, ranging across fields and along known trails through the woods, and had only managed to cover a couple of miles. The temperature was in the teens, and when the wind came up, tree limbs creaked like porch swings on a summer night.

Where a trail emptied into a wide-open field, I stopped at the tree line and leaned against a giant beech to rest. I steadied myself with my poles and took in the down-sloping cornfield where the stubble of cut stalks peeked through the snow. Across the entire landscape, the snow was pristinely smooth and undulating. Farther down was a frozen stream, and beyond that, an old stone house that a Manhattan couple had bought and renovated. Threads of smoke rose from the chimney. From the yard around the house, a small bridge crossed the stream, and then a gap between two rows of slender birches marking the driveway ran along the foot of the cornfield, and continued up a hill to a distant ridge, where the road was.

Snow blew off a nearby pine. I watched it carry in the wind and scatter into dust, and then, as clear as if it were ten feet away, I heard the door on the house open and bang shut. In the cold silence, the sound echoed out of the dell like a gunshot. A figure ran up the unplowed driveway. It was a woman, running and punching herself in the stomach.

I watched in confusion until I realized what was happening. She was choking. Pushing off with my poles, I pumped furiously down the slope, plowing through the deep snow, going as fast as I could without falling, cutting through the cornfield to the driveway. As I skied through the trees, she saw me and grabbed her throat. Her eyes bulged. I pressed the boot-release buttons on my skis, threw down my poles and hurried over to her. Her face was bright pink, her lips were blue. I got behind her, knotted my hands under her sternum and wrenched her off the ground. Nothing happened. I did it again and again. Nothing. She began to thrash. Finally, on the sixth or seventh try, something flew out of her mouth and she sucked in a high-pitched breath.

I still had my arms around her and my pelvis buried against her backside. She heaved air in and out of her lungs. We were both shaking. Somewhere in the distance, a crow cawed. I loosened my grip and noticed how she was dressed, which, I reasoned, might have something to do with her trembling. She wore an apron embroidered with a Currier and Ives print, a thin red T-shirt, black yoga pants and socks without shoes. I let go of her and put a hand on her shoulder.

"Are you okay? You should get inside."

She spun around with tears rolling down her cheeks and hugged me, clung to me, her fingers clawing my ski jacket. As she sobbed into my chest, I noticed faint streaks of silver in her otherwise flawless gold hair. She smelled of ginger.

In the cold stillness her reaction seemed melodramatic, but then again I had never almost choked to death.

"You're okay." I rubbed her back.

She looked up and stared at me. Her eyes were straight out of a fairy tale—enormous and arrestingly blue.

"I thought I was dead. I saw flashes and everything."

"Well, it's over now. Put this on."

I took off my knapsack and lightweight ski jacket and draped the jacket over her shoulders. She scanned the length of the driveway.

"The plow guy should have been here by now." Her voice was pensive.

Springing up on her tiptoes, she hugged me again and this time kissed me, aiming for my cheek but hitting my ear instead. The kiss took me off guard, and by the time it registered, she had already stepped away. She was facing the mountain behind her house, far across the snowy field. She threw her arms out wide and shouted.

"Cookie dough!"

Her breath hung in the frigid air. There was an echo. She spun around and glared defiantly at me.

"I almost died over goddamn cookie dough!"

"I thought you weren't supposed to eat raw cookie dough," I said.

"You're not."

Her cheeks were still wet. She turned in a circle and gazed at the landscape. Suddenly she froze. A look of panic came over her face.

"The cookies!"

She sprinted for the house. My jacket flew off her shoulders and crumpled in the snow.

This was where, if I'd been gallant and selfless and smart, I would have put my jacket back on and skied home. No thank-you, no goodbye, just *go*. Instead, I hesitated. Dusting off the jacket, I made the mistake of glancing at her bounding through the smooth snow. Even in the apron, it was clear she had a taut, petite body underneath that in summer would draw some attention. There was the tang of wood smoke in the air, too, and I was shivering uncontrollably. Surely after saving her life, she wouldn't begrudge me a few minutes' warmth by her fire. I put my jacket on, picked up my skis and poles, and followed her.

She'd left the heavy oak door gaping. Clearly, she meant for me to follow. Smoke poured out of the doorway, along with the sounds of swearing and banging metal. I leaned my skis and poles against the house and kicked the snow off my boots.

"Hello?"

"Dammit! Oh, come in, come in!"

She whirled around holding a smoldering baking sheet in an oven mitt, switched on the stove hood, stomped on a garbage can pedal, and dumped the cookie cinders. It was only once she'd hosed down the baking sheet that it became quiet enough to hear "Baby It's Cold Outside" playing on a stereo somewhere. This part of the house was one large open room. A fire hissed in the fireplace, with three personalized stockings nailed to the wooden mantel: Aldous, Erika and Tyler. In the corner near the fireplace, liquor bottles crowded a small bar cart. I'd been inside all of ten seconds, and the place already felt dangerously warm and comfortable. I started to shut the door.

"Leave it open," she said. "It's the only way to get all the smoke out. Hang up your coat, sit by the fire, please."

I hung it and my knapsack on a hook behind the door, and balanced my hat, mittens and scarf on top.

"Boots, too," she said. "Get comfortable. I'll be right back."

My socks were damp. I eased into a padded rocking chair beside the fire, held my feet out, and looked around. The ceiling beams were heavy and prominent, like in other old houses I'd been in. The kitchen gleamed with green granite countertops and stainless steel appliances. The floors were wide hardwood planks. The sole covering on the floor was an Oriental rug against the far wall, where a Christmas tree, knee-deep in presents, stood to one side of a bay window of paned glass. Each pane formed a small painting of a view of the property: the frozen stream, a split-rail fence, a small apple orchard, a garage designed to resemble an old barn, and a horse sleigh. I had been alone for five or ten minutes when I heard the floorboards creak in the other room and footsteps approach.

"Do you have horses?" I asked aloud.

"What?" she said.

"Your sleigh outside. Ever taken a sleigh ride?"

She came back into the room and closed the front door. Her apron was gone, but she was wearing the same thin red T-shirt and black yoga pants. Maybe she'd needed to change her socks. Her hair was brushed, making her look less frazzled, and her face was less pale than it had been earlier. She had put on makeup.

"Horses?" she said. "Oh, the sleigh? No, that's just decorative. Coffee?"

"Sure."

She set up a coffee tray and brought it over. She laid it on the coffee table between fanned-out copies of the *New Yorker* and *Martha Stewart Living*.

"How do you take it?" she asked.

"Black, thanks."

"Care to make it Irish?"

A grandfather clock in the corner read quarter-past ten.

"Bit early, isn't it?"

She ignored me, went to the bar cart and removed a bottle from the throng: Bushmills Irish Whiskey. Its amber contents sparkled in the firelight. She looked at me for several seconds without blinking—a dramatic gesture considering the enormity of her eyes.

"All right," I said.

"Top o' the mornin' to ya." She poured in whiskey until it spilled over the brim. "Whoops, sorry." She sipped it. Her lips were pink. They looked soft.

"Careful, hot." She handed me the mug.

"Thanks," I said.

She plopped into the love seat next to my rocking chair and curled her legs beneath her. I'd always found this maneuver strangely alluring when performed by svelte women. The love seat had a print of a fox hunt on it.

"So, Erika." I nodded at the stockings. "I'm assuming you're not Aldous."

"No, my husband." She drank some coffee. "It's a family name."

The fire popped.

"Mine's Henry."

"Don't hear that one much anymore," she said.

"It's also a family name."

"Well, Henry, thank you for saving my life. I'd be frozen in a ditch right now if it weren't for you." She held out a plate of cookies. "Gingerbread man? Early batch. Non-incinerated."

"Sure." I took two and bit the leg off one. "You must have been at it for a while. I could smell the ginger on you earlier."

"Oh, did you?" She smirked. "Yes, I've been awake since five, baking up a storm. Nothing else to do."

"For your son's class?"

"Church bake sale." She looked away and shook her head. "We're such hypocrites. We only attend Christmas Eve."

"I'll do you one better—I never go."

"How roguish of you."

She sipped some coffee and locked eyes with me over her steaming mug.

The coffee was potent with whiskey, but I found myself sipping more and more of it. I ate the two cookies and looked around.

"You've done a great job with this place. When I was a boy, this house was just a pile of rocks. Do you know anything about its history?"

"Yes, it belonged to a Tory during the Revolutionary War," she said.

"Come on, how do you know that?"

She put down her mug, sprang off the love seat and beckoned me with a finger.

"Come with me."

I followed her away from the fireplace sitting area to the far wall. She paused beside the big bay window and the Christmas tree, and pointed at a patch of charred stones near the ceiling.

"During the war," she said, "a band of locals torched the place."

"Oh? Was that before or after George Washington slept here?"

"Ha, ha." She sat in the window seat. Some of the panes were frosted over. "Here, sit."

She patted the cushion. I eased down sipping my coffee.

"Need that freshened up?" she asked.

"All right."

Erika whisked away with my mug and returned with both of ours and the whiskey bottle. I swore I could smell the whiskey from two feet away. She handed me mine, put the bottle on the floor, and got into the window seat with me, leaving no space between us.

She leaned against my arm and peered out the window. She was warm and relaxed, like a cat sleeping in a sun patch.

"So, did you grow up around here?"

"Yeah," I said. "The Vale, actually. Just south of Wellington. Know where I'm talking about?"

"Sure." She gestured with her mug. "It's like, over that way."

She was blatantly pressing her body into mine now.

"You must resent city people like us," she said. "Moving up here, buying all the property."

I drank a good slug of the coffee, which, at this point, was like drinking straight Irish whiskey. The smoky taste of the liquor mingled with the faint aroma of wood smoke that permeated everything in this house—the beams, the walls, even Erika. With nothing in my stomach but the two gingerbread men, the Irish "coffee" was hitting me hard. The feeling came on like a head rush: I was gazing outside at the swirling snow, and when I turned back to her, my head swam.

"You okay?" she said.

"Fine. I'm"—I raised my mug—"I'm...not used to this. What were we talking about? Right. No, I don't resent you. You city folks've driven up real estate prices and taxes a bit, that's all."

"I know." She rested her cheek against the window pane. "When we were first looking for property up here, it was so quaint and untouched, I almost didn't want to ruin it. Does that make any sense?"

"Yeah." I pulled my feet up and reclined into a nest of throw pillows. "The area *has* lost some of its wildness. When I was a boy, I could count on one hand the number of cars that went by on the main road."

Erika stretched out next to me, propping herself up on one elbow.

"What about you?" she said. "Doesn't the quiet get to you after a while?"

"No, I love it. Hell, anytime I go down to Manhattan, I don't know what to do with myself. Don't get me wrong, I enjoy it. But all that stimulation—it's overwhelming."

"Well, it's different when you're up here alone."

"All alone?" I said.

"Well, Tyler's here, of course, but he's six and at school all day. And this week, I don't even have him. He's with his grandparents."

She looked at me with those fairy tale princess eyes of hers. I could hear the clock ticking across the room.

"So," I said, "your husband lives in the city during the week? What does he do?"

She drank a swig of coffee like it was a shot, and clapped the mug down on the window ledge.

"Oh, *please*. Do you really give a *damn* what he does?" She grabbed my ring hand and shook it. "What does your *wife* do? What do *you* do? I hate that question. Every party I go to, they all ask it. It's the most inane question there is, frankly."

I smiled. "So you don't like it?"

She took my mug and placed it next to hers. Then, flouncing her hair over her collar, she leaned down and kissed me. The whiskey and coffee were strong on her lips and tongue, although on her the tastes were better and I kissed her harder to get more of them. I caressed her earlobe and felt her quiver. As I slid my hand under her T-shirt and traced one of the bra cups with my fingers,

I noticed that the Christmas music had stopped, leaving only the hiss and pop of the fire across the room. The window panes rattled from the wind outside. The sudden stillness in the house made me acutely aware of the absurdity of the situation: it wasn't 11 a.m. yet, I was nearly drunk, and I had my hand up the shirt of a housewife I'd met less than an hour ago. I removed my hand.

"Why don't we go for a walk?" I said.

She groaned. "But it's freezing out there. And it's so snuggly in here, next to you."

"Well, I need some air."

I stood.

"Fine."

She sat up and grabbed the whiskey bottle. Ten seconds later she stood at the front door in shearling boots and a white down ski jacket. I put on my ski boots.

"Aren't you going to wear a hat?" I asked.

"Nah, screw it. Let's go!"

Outside, it had begun to storm again, with the snow blowing sideways in gusts. We put an arm around each other, passed the bottle back and forth, and cut a serpentine path around the garage-barn. We went through a break in the rail fence and over a footbridge across the frozen stream. Where the stream widened out, there was a small pond with a bench. I sipped some whiskey. My face was hot now and I could feel the snow melting as it hit my cheeks.

"Do you folks ice-skate?" I asked.

"Nope."

"Tell me you at least have a snowmobile. With all this property, I mean. What is this, fifty acres?"

"A hundred, and nope, no snowmobile." She grabbed the bottle and took a swig, then leapt on me and kissed me. Even though she was a tiny thing, I almost fell over.

"You *saved* me, Henry! I nearly choked to death. What a horrible way to die."

"You're okay now." I put her down.

"Yeah, I'm *great*. Just wonderful."

She marched across the field ahead of me, her white jacket almost invisible in the storm. All I could see distinctly were her shearling boots, kicking up the snow. She looked over her shoulder and waved me forward. Her hair was white with snow.

"Come on, country boy!"

I caught up to her. "Where are we going?"

"Who cares? Anywhere but here." She shoved the bottle into my ribs.

"No, I've had enough," I said. "One of us has to walk us home."

She threw her head back as though it were on a hinge and laughed into the sky. Then she stopped, blinked at me through the snow and said, "You won't leave me alone this winter, will you, Henry?"

"Of course not."

"Maybe you'll take me for a sleigh ride?"

"You bet."

Swaying on her feet, she tried chugging the rest of the whiskey, but coughed it over her jacket. The bottle slipped out of her hand. As she bent over for it, I grabbed her arm.

"Okay, Erika. You've had enough. Let's go back."

She jerked her arm away and ran across the field, slipping every few steps, laughing, then slipping again and laughing harder. She was heading for the pond.

"Erika, stop!"

"Don't tell me what to do!"

I ran as fast as I could in the deep snow with ski boots on and caught up to her as she stepped on the ice. I grabbed her around the waist. Once we were safely across the footbridge she stopped struggling and instead leaned into me, holding my arm around her.

"Let's go in," I said. "I'll make you hot chocolate."

"Cocoa? Yes! And I'm going to eat *all* the cookies! Screw the church."

We reached the garage. This time when she leapt up and threw her arms and legs around me, I was somehow ready for it, clenching her petite backside and kissing her as I staggered through the snow. At the corner of the house, I felt myself starting to sweat from the exertion and pressed her back against the stones to rest my legs. Her fingers were in my hair, on my neck, inside my coat and heading south. I heard a low rumble in the distance.

"Erika." I opened one eye to see a red GMC pickup growling around the bend in the driveway, plowing a path straight for the house. I shoved her off me. Erika wiped her mouth with the back of her hand.

"Crap," she said. "I forgot about him."

It was Craig Thompson, a casual friend of mine and a fixture in Wellington. Like every other country contractor with a pickup truck, Craig supplemented his winter income by snowplowing. He rolled down his window and gave me a tiny nod. Erika stayed put while I walked over to the truck.

"Hello, Erika," he said over my shoulder.

"Hello, Craig."

"Henry," he said. "How goes it?"

"Hey, you must be busy, huh? What's the word on this storm?"

"Supposed to go all day and all night. Give you a lift home?"

He took a Winston from a pack on the dashboard. He lighted it with a kitchen match off his thumbnail, and tossed the match in the ashtray.

"Hey, those'll kill you," I said.

He took a drag and flicked the ash in Erika's direction. "So will those."

I lowered my voice and leaned in the window. "I just met her, Craig. This is going to sound ridiculous, but I was skiing by earlier and she ran out of her house *choking*. I had to give her the Heimlich, right there in the driveway."

"I bet."

"I'm not kidding, Craig. She's just lonely."

"They all are, Henry. They all are." He put the truck in drive. "Be careful's all I'm sayin'."

"Yeah."

I stood at the front door with Erika and watched him plow the rest of the driveway. He did it in less than ten minutes, honking on his way out. I waved. Erika nudged me.

"What'd he say?"

"Nothing."

"Come on, then—cocoa," she said.

"We should probably call it a day," I said. "Besides, we've got all winter, right?"

"Please, I don't want to be alone today. I don't care what some woodchuck thinks."

"Easy, he's a friend."

She hugged me, looked up at me with the full force of her hypnotic blue eyes.

"I've got a four-poster bed in there that doesn't see enough action," she said. "Not nearly enough. Canopy and everything. Oh, and there's a working fireplace in the bedroom. We could have a fire and—"

"Erika, I have to go." I unhooked her arms. "We had a fun time today. Let's not ruin it."

"At least come in for cocoa."

"Look," I said, "you're drunk, I'm drunk, and I need some time to process this. This whole situation with you—I didn't expect it."

"When will you be back?"

"Give me a day or two. But next time, don't be choking, okay?"

"I won't," she said. "Wait, your knapsack!"

She popped inside and came back out with it.

"Thanks." I took the knapsack and kissed her once on the mouth. "Now get inside and warm up. I'll see you soon."

I put on my skis, looped my mittens through the pole straps, and started up the drive. Then I cut into the cornfield where I had broken trail earlier and herringbone-stepped to the top. At the giant beech tree, I looked back and barely made her out through the falling snow. She hadn't moved from her spot in front of the house. She looked like a snow sculpture. Unsure if she could see me or not, I raised a mitten to wave, and at precisely that moment she came to life and went inside, shutting the door behind her.

The wind gusted in my face on the way home, and the new snow had partially covered my trail. By the time I got home, the two-mile trek felt like five, but I had had a chance to think.

The next morning, I decided to walk to Erika's. I was walking along the shoulder and mulling the situation when Craig pulled over.

"Give you a lift?"

I got in and waited until he pulled away before speaking.

"I'm breaking it off with her," I said.

"Best thing."

"Not that we did anything. We just met yesterday. I mean, I think I should do it in person, make sure she understands, you know?"

"Have to." He loosened his fingers on the steering wheel and re-gripped it. "Only way to know she gets the message and won't pull any surprises."

"Wise man, Craig."

At her mailbox, he turned into the driveway and dropped the plow. Ten inches of fresh snow had accumulated since yesterday. The sun was bright and glared fiercely off the snow.

"Might as well take you down. Got to plow here anyway."

"Thanks."

"This way, you can make it quick," he said. "I'll wait for you."

"Good idea."

"I'll make a pass down to the garage first."

At the end of the driveway, he rammed the snow toward the sleigh and started backing up when I spotted something.

"Hold it!"

He stopped the truck. "What?"

"There, look!" I pointed at the garage. Smoke rose from cracks in the sliding door. "Something's burning!"

I jumped out, ran to the door and hauled it open. A miasma of smoke engulfed me. Somewhere in the dense fog, an engine ran. I started coughing uncontrollably. I was stumbling outside when Craig flew by me and disappeared into the cloud. A door opened and the engine shut off. He came out holding his breath and shaking his head. Fumes trailed behind him. Several yards into the driveway, he rested his hands on his knees and gasped.

"Jesus," he said.

"Was she—"

"Yeah, it's her all right."

"Oh, shit."

We stood in the long shadow of the garage, squinting out at the field, where the new snow had covered my and Erika's footsteps. Just the day before, I had walked with her and kissed her. Now that I thought about it, there had been something haunting and desperate about her laugh. Why hadn't I noticed it yesterday?

"So," Craig said, standing up. "How do you want to play this, Henry?"

"What do you mean?"

"I *mean*, I doubt anybody knows you were here yesterday—besides me, that is—and if...well, this whole thing could get pretty messy."

"I'm not going to pretend this didn't happen. When the cops get here, I'll explain everything."

"There's nothing incriminating inside, is there?" He looked at me, the house, then me again. "Did you..."

"Have sex with her? No, Craig, I didn't."

"All right. My phone's in the truck."

I waited outside while he went back in the truck cab and made the call. After I caught my breath, I got in the cab with him, and we sat without saying anything. Half an hour passed like that, until a state police SUV turned into the driveway on top of the ridge. Craig lit a cigarette and cracked his window.

"Damn. Another sad, rich broad." He exhaled through his nose. "I mean, come on, what's she got to be sad about? Nice-looking woman, cute kid, plenty of money, this place, apartment in Manhattan—the woman had it all." Craig shook his head. "Sometimes I just don't know."

I stared at the open garage door, where the fumes had cleared out enough to see her. Her face was a pale glacier blue, and she was slumped behind the wheel of a Porsche SUV.

8

SCORNED WOMEN

Upon opening his eyes that Saturday morning, Jimmy Tatko experienced a clarity and sense of peace that he hadn't felt since he was a boy.

And for the first time in months, there was no pain. None.

The herniated disc from a fall off some scaffolding two years ago wasn't throbbing. His right knee and shoulder didn't ache. And that faint sense in his abdomen, his chest, his neck and his head that something invasive was in there, something like ivy slowly choking his organs, sucking the damn life out of him—well, miraculously, that was gone, too.

Jimmy rose slowly, convinced that any second one of his many pains would strike. He showered, put on his robe and switched on the coffee maker. By the time he poured himself a cup and went out on the deck, he was moving with his usual laid-back swagger.

The air was cold. He could see his breath. He loved that sour smell of the leaf tannin this time of year. After weeks of unseasonable heat, the fall was finally here. The days were cooler, the leaves were nearing their peak color.

He'd always risen early, of course—to get to job sites—but today, for the first time in years, he took a moment to experience that magic hour between night and sunrise. He could see the start of the sunrise, yet still make out the stars. There was something on the horizon too big and bright to be a star. One of the planets, maybe, but which one? Venus? It bothered him that in almost 36 years he hadn't bothered to learn more about the planets. An impulse rose up in him to rush inside and do an internet search, but he stopped himself. He had something more important to do today, something that could *only* be done today.

Inside, Jimmy poured the rest of the coffee in a Thermos and got dressed in the ridiculous fox-hunting outfit: the white breeches that made his bulge look like he was packing a beanbag down there, the heavy wool scarlet coat, and the black riding boots. Everything fit a lot more snugly than he was used to, and he was convinced he looked like a fool. But when he put the helmet on and appraised himself in the mirror, he was surprised by how natural he looked. In the brilliant red coat it was easy to imagine himself as one of the hilltoppers, and not merely the carpenter who built their homes. He raised his jaw the way Hamilton Highgate and John Hammersley did when they spoke to him.

"Not bad, Jimmy," he said to himself. "Not bad."

He shut out the light, grabbed his coffee, keys and Thermos, and went out to the truck. The sky became pink as the engine warmed, and by the time the clock on the dashboard read 7:02, he couldn't see the stars or Venus anymore.

By tradition, on the day of the Wellington Hunt all landowners opened their properties to members of the Hunt—in effect to anyone on a horse in fox-hunting attire. It was the one day of the year that Jimmy would have unfettered access to all of the estates—something he needed in order to talk to all of the women he had in mind. He'd been trying to talk to each of them for six months, but none would see him. In the village, they avoided him. Their driveway gates, even the service entrances, were closed to him. But today, if his plan went well, he would be able to see and talk to most of them in one fell swoop. Besides opening their fence gates, most of the women on his list would be hosting parties. Even when they discovered Jimmy was an impostor, they couldn't throw him out. Tradition prevented it.

Jimmy sipped some coffee and put the pickup into drive. The cleverness of his plan pleased him, as did the knowledge that it was inspired by a private passion. Ever since Mrs. G's class in high school, Jimmy had been quietly obsessed with American literature, reading a book a week—at home, or in his truck during lunch breaks. Only his daughter, the village librarians and Natasha Hammersley knew his secret. His favorite book was *The Stories of John Cheever*, and he had read two of the stories at least dozen times, as though they contained coded clues to buried treasure: "The Swimmer," in which a man named Neddy Merrill goes home by swimming his neighbor's pools across the county, and "The Chaste Clarissa," in which a rake named Baxter seduces a smoking hot, married redhead. Reading "Clarissa" again last week, Jimmy experienced a flush of regret at how many times he had behaved similarly. The stories got him thinking. He wanted to make amends with the women he'd wronged, and like Neddy in "The Swimmer" he wanted to do it with panache; but instead of going from estate to estate around Wellington swimming, he'd ride a horse.

With the sun piercing the woods now, he could see the vivid color on the hillsides surrounding the village, and the beauty of it made his eyes water. The fall had been his favorite season since he was a young boy. At that time, Jimmy had foreseen an unbroken chain of autumns stretching into infinity. Then, when he hit 30 years old, it occurred to him that if he was lucky he might live to see forty to fifty more. Now, with his latest and final diagnosis, it was just the one. This one. The last one.

Before he met Stephen to pick up the horse, he wanted to swing by the country club. Carmel Cruickshank, the kooky bitch, played golf every morning at dawn, before she would be exposed to direct sunlight. Making the turn into the village, he glanced out at the 14th fairway. Despite her infamously fast-paced game, it was too early for her to be this far along. She might be on the 4th, maybe the 5th, hole. Jimmy took the dirt service road that wended along the course perimeter, and peered through the trees at the tee box on 10 and the pond on 6. He parked behind the 5th green, got out of the truck and walked through the trees. It was still cold, and the green was covered in dew. From the green, he marched down the rough, toward the tee on 5. About 200 yards ahead, the course doglegged, so Jimmy couldn't see if Carmel and her caddy were in the fairway yet or not. The time on his phone read 7:30. Already he was running late. He kept walking.

A 510-yard par-5, this was considered an impossible hole, but Jimmy had mastered it. During the Wellington Country Club Championship this summer, he'd made a birdie here that won him the cup. Jimmy looked out into the fairway. His second shot on this hole, the one that had hooked gorgeously around the dogleg, landed about *there.* Maybe 180 from the pin. Jimmy stepped a few yards into the fairway, took up his stance with an imaginary 3-wood, and swung. That day, Jimmy had swept that ball cleanly off the turf. The ball sailed high, with the perfect arc associated with long football passes, bounced onto the green, struck the pin, and vanished into the hole like a mouse. It was the best shot of his life. Yet remembering it made him think about what might have been: how he might have become a professional golfer if he'd had some self-discipline. He was born with an immense talent, a talent which he'd taken for granted.

So much time. So much wasted, wasted time. If only he'd known how little time he really had, he would have worked harder. He would have treated women better. He would have let his brain guide him instead of his groin.

Once he was around the dogleg, heading toward the 5th tee, Jimmy spotted a Monarch butterfly floundering on the short grass. It was trying to fly but was getting only a few inches in the air before falling again. Something in its movements—the weak flutter of its wings or its tottering crawl between attempts—told Jimmy that the insect was dying. Of course he'd seen insects suffer and die before, and had himself killed more than his share of flies and hornets, but today this butterfly's plight stirred up an emotion unusual for him—pity. Studying its tiny head, Jimmy became conscious of the life in it, and that despite its small size, it was as alive as he was. He got to one knee and held out his hand. The butterfly touched the calluses on his fingers with its antennae and recoiled.

"I won't hurt you," he said softly, surprising himself by speaking to it. "Come on."

To his delight, it crawled into Jimmy's palm, lowered its wings, and appeared to lie down, as though to take a nap. Jimmy slowly stood and tread down the fairway with his palm cradled against his chest. Every so often, the butterfly waved its wings.

There was movement ahead on the 5th tee: two figures in head-to-toe white, and Carmel Cruickshank was one of them. She was easily recognized. In addition to always wearing all-white golf attire, she never drove a cart, instead employing one of the caddies, whose job it was to carry her clubs and to hold a golf umbrella over her once the sun came over the horizon. As a result, the woman was paler than a cameo. Jimmy had been with many tanned women, but he'd found the pale ones sexier for some reason. Obviously Carmel was on this list, and so was Natasha Hammersley. Correction—Natasha was top on the list.

No sooner had he started toward the edge of the fairway than a pink golf ball landed with a plop six feet away. Incredibly close, in fact—as if Carmel had been aiming for him.

His boots were covered with grass clippings, and for some reason this made him think about the time. It was 7:44. Trying to see Carmel this morning was a mistake, but he was already here, and Carmel, wearing a snow-white sweater and golf pants, was less than 100 yards away and closing.

"Get out of the fairway, you idiot!" She brandished her club. "This isn't part of the damn Hunt!"

When they were about 50 yards apart, she squinted at him.

"Oh, it's *you*."

Jimmy stopped. Carmel adjusted her Wellington Country Club baseball cap and brushed by, averting her eyes.

"I'd like to talk to you," he said. "Do you have a few minutes?"

"Does it look like I do? Go away. You're ruining my game, jerk."

Jimmy walked alongside the caddy, took the golf bag from him and slipped it over his own shoulder. At the rattle of clubs, the butterfly stirred, then settled into his hand again.

"Cooper," he said, "meet her at the 6th tee, okay?"

"Mrs. Cruickshank?"

She glanced over her shoulder. "Yes, fine, Cooper, go ahead. Look behind 5, would you? I lost a Pink Lady there yesterday."

"Yes, ma'am."

The caddy peeled off into the rough. As Carmel slowed down, her eyes flicked to the butterfly.

"Who's your little friend?"

"Found him a few minutes ago, in the middle of the fairway."

"So," she said, "Jimmy Tatko rescues insects, and he's riding in the Hunt this morning. Aren't you just *full* of surprises." She slid her club in the bag. "Now what are you doing here? What do you *want*, Jimmy?"

When he was planning this day, Jimmy focused on the *logistics* of seeing all of the women on his list and gave little thought to what he would say to each of them. Foolishly he had imagined the right words would flow out of him. But the words weren't flowing. He had to think. Carmel stood behind her ball with her hands on her hips and stared out at the dogleg.

"You're the expert on this hole," she said. "What do you suggest?"

He was glad that Carmel had changed the subject. He stepped closer to her and pointed down the fairway.

"Well, for starters, don't even *think* of trying to hook around the dogleg or go over those trees. You'll never make it. If I were you, I'd play a 5-iron and lay up at the turn. Then you'll have a clear shot to the pin and a good chance to make par."

He watched her staring out at the dewy, gray-green course. The tiptops of the trees were beginning to glow with the sunrise. Carmel nodded at the big yellow maple at the corner.

"I can clear that," she said. "I've done it before."

"You're making a mistake."

"*Mistake?*"

She marched back to him, stopped a foot away and looked him in the eyes for the first time since he'd dumped her for Caprice Highgate. (Caprice was gone now, and nobody—not even Hamilton—knew where she went.) Carmel tilted her head back until her coppery eyes were distinct beneath the cap brim.

"I'll tell you what the *mistake* is—that I ever took up with you, asshole." She yanked her 3-wood out of the bag, hitting him in the shoulder with the handle.

"Easy, Carmel. Don't disturb the butterfly."

She whipped around so fast that for a second he thought she might be swinging the club at his head.

"The fucking butterfly's dead, Jimmy." She extended her gloved finger for the butterfly to crawl onto. She poked it, and when it didn't move, she picked it up and flung it.

It spiralled to the grass and landed in a divot.

"See?" she said. "Dead."

Jimmy gazed at the butterfly with a bizarrely poignant sense of loss, but he couldn't grieve for long. His attention was drawn to Carmel, who had stepped up to her pink ball, and without so much as a practice swing, wound up and hit the ball with a perfect *thwack!* off the club face, the ball climbing and climbing, then cresting, falling, skimming the top leaves, and disappearing on the other side of the dogleg.

"Nice shot," he said. "You probably landed in the rough, but—"

"The *rough* my ass, Jimmy." She slammed her club back into the bag. "*What* do you want? *Why* are you here? You know I'm out here at dawn every day. This is *my* time on the course, and you're screwing it up."

"I'm here...I want to apologize."

"For?"

"The way things ended between us. For Caprice, for everything."

"*Ended* between us? There was no end. One day you're fucking me with that kielbasa between your legs, and the next day you don't show. You don't call. You avoid me. Nothing *ended*. You were too much of a chickenshit to *end* anything. That would require a semblance of maturity and responsibility—two qualities which we both know you are sorely lacking."

Jimmy checked his phone: 8:02. Damn—now he really was late.

"I'm sorry," he said. "That's what I came here to say. Maybe this was a mistake. I should go."

"You're not even going to caddy the rest of this hole for me? You're *sorry*? Get out of here, you piece of—I'll carry my own clubs." She wrenched the bag off his shoulder.

"Carmel, I'm really sorry about how I treated you. You're a great woman and a great golfer and great in the sack and I'm sorry, but I have to go."

He jogged around the dogleg turn, and when he saw that her ball had landed in the rough, he kicked it into the fairway.

Just as he reached the pair of sandtraps 25 yards before the hole, a ball whizzed by him—near enough that he could actually hear the hiss it made through the air—bounced, and rolled toward the green. Jimmy turned around. In the distance, Carmel was waving at him like Queen Elizabeth II.

———◆———

When he turned into the Highgates' back field, the clock on the dash read 8:22. He was over twenty minutes late.

Stephen was standing beneath a tree, smoking a cigarette. A large, dark horse stood beside him. From the open fence gate, the grass-striped lane sloped up between two rows of old maples and at the top of the hill seemed to vanish. Jimmy got out with his helmet and Thermos.

"You're late, Jimmy." Stephen dropped the cigarette and crushed it under his boot. "I've got a dozen horses to tack up this morning."

"I know, I'm sorry. Had to make a pit stop."

"Whatever. Here." He opened a map and gave it to Jimmy to hold. "Topographical map of Wellington. I've labeled about a dozen estates. They're all supposed to have bright orange signs for the Hunt at their fence gates, with the name of the property owner. If you don't see one, look for 'No Trespassing' signs."

"Really, Stephen, is that what I should do?"

"Screw you." Stephen took a breath, gazed at the hedgerows far across the field. "Over there—that's where Caprice shot those coyotes. She was a real piece of work, huh?"

"Yeah," Jimmy said.

"God, I envy you." Stephen removed the horse's reins from a low tree branch and walked the horse over to Jimmy. "I wanted to nail Caprice so bad. You gotta tell me, Jimmy—was she good? I know you don't like to kiss and tell, and I appreciate that, but just this once, for me? I have to know."

The truth was, most of the women of Wellington he'd bedded—especially the hilltoppers—weren't particularly skilled or experienced when he started with them, but by the end they were both. In fact, by the end many of them had turned into clingy, insatiable harlots, calling him over at all hours, arranging riskier and riskier meetings, coming on to him in stores in the village.

One of them—a seemingly prim newlywed, active in the Episcopal church—had tried to blow him in the back room of the village thrift store. When this sort of thing happened, Jimmy knew it was time to put a stop to it and move on.

Regarding Stephen's question, Jimmy considered telling him the truth—that as of the early summer, when he and Caprice were still screwing three times a week, she had reached a level of proficiency in bed that made Jimmy crave *her*—to the point that he was shamelessly propositioning her at Bendini's with packages of Italian sausage. But he knew Stephen would brood about her if he told him the truth, so he lied.

"Honestly?" he said.

"Yeah, tell me."

Stephen's eyes were as big as an owl's, and his mouth was slack, clearly anticipating a lot of salivating details.

"Great body," Jimmy said, "but she laid there like a rug. One of the most *boring* lays ever."

"*What?*" he said. "A gal like that, I would have thought…oh, well, she's gone now, right?"

He handed Jimmy the reins. The horse turned its head and blinked at him, as though to size him up. Stephen mentioned the horse's name, but Jimmy didn't understand him, and he didn't feel like asking him to repeat it.

"Nice old gal," Stephen continued. "Used to do dressage. Won a few. Please take it easy with her, though. Nothing more than a canter, okay?" He nodded at Jimmy's hands. "A *Thermos?*"

"Yeah, so?"

Stephen grabbed it from him. "You're not on the friggen roundup here, Jimmy. You're riding English. You told me you've done this before."

"I have."

"All right. Truck keys?"

Jimmy handed them to him and brought the reins back to the saddle. He put on his helmet and fastened it.

"Crap on your boots?" Stephen asked. "Check."

"Clean."

Stephen laced his fingers together. Jimmy put his left boot in Stephen's hands, pushed and swung his right leg over. A shooting pain zapped through his abdomen and up his spine.

The pain was back.

"Remember," Stephen said, "lower barn—the one on Celia's side of the property. *Before* sunset. I'll have your truck there."

"Got it. Thanks."

"Where you headed first?"

Jimmy shrugged. "I figured long as I'm over here, I'd go north of the village first."

Stephen nodded. "Got your phone?"

"Right here." He patted his coat pocket.

"You look like a dweeb, by the way," Stephen said. "You're going to fit right in today."

Jimmy snorted. "You know what, Stephen? I lied about Caprice." He wheeled the horse around. "She was one of the best ever. Nearly passed out when I came with her—several times in fact."

"You prick," Stephen said.

Jimmy cupped his crotch. "That's right, Stevie. A big one."

He trotted up the lane beneath the trees, and at the next open gate, crossed the road onto an old rail bed.

———————•◆•———————

The railroad bed ran behind the shooting club. It wasn't nine o'clock yet, and already there were enough shotguns blasting simultaneously to make it sound like there was a Civil War skirmish going on in the woods. He stopped the horse, pulled out the topographical map and formed a plan of attack. He would work his way in a clockwise circle—north to east to south to west—around the township, a route that would take him to the six scorned women in this order: Ginny Warburton, Shannon Childs, Natasha Hammersley (what would he say to *her*?), Caterina Orlando, Gillian Barnes, and Leah Gold. Since he had no idea how long it would take to ride from estate to estate, he needed to keep each visit short. There were half a dozen other women he would have liked to speak with, including Camille Van Ness, Jaclyn Urquhart and Sylvia Kirkland, but they were all out of town this weekend. There were a lot of women to see today, and a lot of ground to cover, and even though he'd already seen Carmel, he needed to be efficient. Ginny's estate was the most remote, and it would take a while to get there. He headed out.

He followed the rail bed for several miles until it passed through a rock cut, and soon Jimmy came to a dirt road that crossed the tracks. He turned down the road, and the horse, as if sensing that time was a factor today, went into a trot. At first Jimmy jounced in the saddle, until he remembered that he was supposed to move up and down in time with the horse's gait. Posting, they called it. He passed a phone booth and continued down the road. Ahead was the old Finishing School, abandoned for 40 years and now surrounded by chain-link fence. Jimmy remembered a couple of beer parties they'd had in there. How the chalkboards had had 40-year-old assignments written on them, how the library still had books in it, and how the art studio still had dozens of student paintings. All of the buildings were scheduled for demolition sometime during the winter. Jimmy wondered if he'd still be alive when that happened. He was getting the hang of posting again when the road dead-ended. He stopped and checked the map. A path continued through a trampled thicket.

He clucked the horse down a steep slope. There was a brook at the bottom. He forded it. Walking purposefully forward, the horse seemed to have been here before, Jimmy thought—a thought confirmed when he saw a fence with an open gate, and an orange sign that read, "WARBURTON — WELCOME!" The paper rattled in the breeze. Beyond the fence was a sweeping field, and in the distance, standing on a hill, was a mammoth white Dutch Colonial.

It was Ginny's house, all right—with that unsightly pool wing protruding from one end.

Trotting up the field, he could see no activity on this side of the house, although as he followed the driveway a truck from Brittany's Gourmet Catering rumbled past. When he reached the top and steered around a copse of trees, there was a large tent. Bales of hay and buckets of water sat beneath the awning. A young man in a tweed hunting jacket and jodhpurs jogged out of the tent smiling.

"I'll take care of her, sir." He craned his neck down the hill. "And where is the rest of your party?"

"There isn't one." Jimmy dismounted and checked his phone. It was 9:40.

"I'm sorry, sir?" the groom said.

"I'm it," he said. "*Alone.*"

When he said this, across the tent Ginny Warburton whipped her head around. She wore a tweed hunting outfit like the groom's, but with her blonde hair in a bun and the glasses, she looked like a lonely man's fantasy of a librarian. She scowled in his direction, then, as if a pleasant thought had come over her, walked over and kissed him on the cheek.

"James! It's wonderful to see you! Come inside, please. You're early, but we have coffee and pastries and Bloody Marys and mimosas. Come!" She hooked her arm around his with a firmness that felt like a jujitsu hold. They crunched across the driveway toward the front door.

"How are you, Ginny?" he asked.

"Oh, me? Great, just great. There are some people I want you to meet."

Something about her nonchalance felt forced. This wasn't the overdramatic Ginny he knew.

"I need to talk to you alone," he said.

"Do you? Well, maybe later."

She took him inside. The house hadn't changed at all since her divorce. The foyer had the same soulless antiques, in the same places, and the terrace outside was visible through a pair of archways that led through the middle of the house to the back. The French doors were open. Still gripping his arm, she walked him outside.

A dozen people were on the terrace. Men read newspapers beneath an umbrella, others grazed at the buffet, and the women lay on chaises. They were all drinking Bloody Marys or Mimosas, and none of them wore hunting attire. In fact, some of them looked like they had just rolled out of bed. Jimmy felt conspicuously overdressed.

"*Everyone*," Ginny said, drawing out the word, "I'd like you to meet James Francis Tatko, the man I was stupidly screwing, which caused William to divorce me! Everyone, say hello to James."

Nobody said anything. Newspapers rustled. The women sipped their drinks. One of the women eyed Jimmy's groin and whispered to the woman next to her.

"That's right, Stephanie," Ginny said. "Equipment-wise, James here is blessed. And it was *so* worth losing William over, without a doubt."

Jimmy gritted his teeth. The melodramatic bitch was still clutching his arm as tightly as a tourniquet. She handed him a Mimosa and took a Bloody Mary for herself.

"Oh, James," she said, "you're as red as your coat. No need to be modest, dear."

One of the women stirred her Bloody Mary with a celery stalk. She was one of those gorgeous Mediterranean women cursed with a prominent nose, as though the gods had decided to modestly deface her to give other women a fighting chance.

"What do you do, James?" she asked.

"Well, I—"

"You mean *besides* pound women like a well drill, Porchia?" Ginny said. "He's a carpenter, and a damn good one, I hate to admit it. Yes, if you want to build an addition, put in kitchen cabinets, or be fucked silly until you lose your husbands…girls, James is your man."

One of the men glanced over his shoulder at Jimmy. He frowned and turned back to his *New York Times*. Jimmy wanted to pull away from Ginny, but he couldn't do it without shoving her. He put down the Mimosa. Ginny drank half of her Bloody Mary, then said, "I haven't told you all the best part. When your husband leaves and you need James, he'll already be gone, on to—or should I say *on top of?*—another woman. No messy emotional attachments, no crying on the phone, none of that." She took another sip of her drink and nudged him with her glass. "Go on, James, show them. Girls, get ready to faint. Go on, James, show them your—"

He wrenched Ginny around and hauled her into the house with him.

"I wasn't finished," she said.

"Shut up."

He dragged her through the kitchen, through the great room, down the long hallway, and into the pool room. The pool room was all glass, and the still water reflected the trees outside. Ginny pried loose from him, pushing him away. She sat down on the diving board. Her glasses were askew.

"Tell me you were at least a little embarrassed," she said.

"I was."

"Mortified?"

"Yes, mortified."

"Good." She straightened her glasses. "Now you know how I feel."

"I was an absolute bastard to you," he said. "I admit it."

She sniffed and held the backs of her hands against her eyes.

"I am *not* going to cry. You're not worth it."

He resisted the urge to sigh and stared at the pool water instead. It was only a couple of years ago when he would come over Monday mornings, after William left for the city, and the two of them swam here in the nude and went at it in the shallow end like…well…like otters, if they copulated a lot. Ginny sniffed. The sound echoed in the big, empty room.

"Why are you here anyway, James? And what is *this* all about?" She pinched his coat.

"I'm here to apologize."

"Apologize? You ruined my life!"

"Come on, Ginny. Don't turn this into one of your soap operas."

Looking up from the cement, she glanced at him, then the door. She stood, removed her glasses, folded them and carefully slid them in her jacket pocket. Standing in front of him, maybe six feet away, she unbuttoned the jacket and started on her blouse.

"Ginny, what are you doing?"

Expressionless, as if in a trance, she laid the tweed jacket on the diving board, then took off her blouse and draped it on top of the jacket. Jimmy turned his head away. Rather than arousing him, Ginny's strip show was having the opposite effect. He backed up toward the door.

"Ginny, I don't have time for this."

Sitting on the diving board, she shucked off the boots, then peeled off everything else until she was nude.

She ran to the shallow end and jumped in, craning her neck to keep her hair from getting wet, then dog-paddled to the deep end, where he was, and held onto the cement edge by her curled fingertips. She smiled wickedly.

"You have time," she said.

Her breasts were wet and slippery-looking. Ordinarily, at this point Jimmy would already be in the pool with her, doing what the two of them had done a hundred times before, but this was no ordinary day. He *had* to get around to all of the women on his list—especially Natasha.

"I'm sorry, Ginny, but I really don't."

As the door was closing behind him, he heard her muttering, "Stupid bitch. When will you ever learn?"

———————◆———————

When he got back on the horse, it was 10:30. The sun was bright, but the air was still cool—in the low 50s, Jimmy figured. In the distance he heard the sound of yelping hounds. The Warburton estate bordered a dirt road that led straight to the next woman on his list, Shannon Childs. A mile or two in the distance, several colorful hot air balloons drifted along the ridge line, some of them precariously close to the trees. The balloons were another Hunt tradition: hilltoppers hired them so their Manhattan guests could take in the "action" and the foliage.

Jimmy rode on, watching the balloons as they floated out of sight, until he reached the Childs' driveway.

Ultramodern, the Childs' house seemed to go on forever down the hill: it was composed of multiple buildings connected by glass breezeways. There was no activity around the place except for a man with a leaf blower. Jimmy dismounted, tied the horse to a small tree and wandered down the hill. The pool was covered, and a sagging badminton net was set up on the lawn off to the side. Jimmy walked toward the man with the leaf blower.

"Hello!" he shouted. "Hello!"

The man saw him and cut the motor. He removed the ear protectors from one of his ears.

"Is Mrs. Childs at home?" Jimmy asked.

The man opened his mouth and was about to say something when he saw something over Jimmy's shoulder. He restarted the leaf blower and walked away.

It was Mr. Childs, rounding the corner of the house. The balding, aging sawed-off, perpetually angry about the three physical conditions over which he had no control, marched across the grass. He had an argyle sweater draped over his shoulders and carried a steaming mug, held away from his body as if it contained a caustic potion.

When he was still 50 feet away, he said, "Why are you—look, we're not *doing* the horse thing this year. The Hammersleys are having…"

Jimmy took off his helmet. The riding had made him sweat, and the breeze was cool on his forehead. Childs had halted a safe distance away. The man's breathing was deep, his eyes enormous. Jimmy stood absolutely still.

He felt like he'd disturbed a rattlesnake. The drone of the leaf blower faded down the hill.

"You," Childs said. He took a step forward. Then another. There was a hypnotic slowness to his movements. "*You*," he said again.

"I made a wrong turn," Jimmy said. "I'll leave."

He started back up the hill, and Childs cut him off.

"I can't *believe* you," he said. "Here to fuck Shannon again?"

"Listen, I made a mis—"

Out of the corner of his eye, Jimmy caught a glimpse of an amber-colored spray in midair before it splashed into the side of his face and neck. The scalding sensation was so intense, he could have sworn his skin was melting off. He couldn't breathe. He felt his mouth open but couldn't form words. There was only the pain, which, instead of dissipating, intensified. Jimmy careened sideways holding his palm against his face like he'd been hit with a boxer's right hook. He tripped into a flowerbed beside the house. The soil was cool where it stuck to his opposite cheek.

When he caught his breath, he didn't yell. He didn't say a word. In fact, he was shocked by how calm he was.

Jimmy pushed himself up and got unsteadily to his feet. He made a fist and looked around. Childs had backed up to the corner of the house and wielded the empty mug as if he would strike Jimmy with it if he came any closer. Jimmy walked toward him anyway. Then Shannon ran over from the pool patio and snatched the mug away from her husband.

"Stop it, Terence! Right now!"

The burning on the side of Jimmy's face had made him lightheaded and dreamy. The lawn looked like one unbroken green carpet. Somewhere, someone was burning leaves. And then he noticed tall and willowy Shannon, in short-shorts and green Hunter Wellies, standing beside her stocky husband. She looked like a fresh sapling growing beside a stump. Shannon winced when she looked at Jimmy.

"Jesus Christ, Terence! What did you do? Jimmy, are you okay?" She approached him cautiously. "Let me see. Oooh…not good. Terence, go get a towel and ice—no, a cold wet towel and some frozen vegetables."

"I'm not helping him," Terence said. "I should have thrown it in his goddamn crotch."

"Please, Terence."

"Bitch." He stormed into the house.

Shannon led Jimmy by the arm to a pair of chaises beside the pool. "Lie down." She patted the headrest of one and dragged the other close to it.

"I'll sit here," she said.

The skin on his face and neck was buzzing, but it only hurt when he touched it.

Golden leaves from a nearby ash tree coated the pool cover like glitter. To the east, a hot air balloon with a swirling red-and-white pattern drifted down behind the ridge. Jimmy was watching it disappear when a wet towel landed on the cement beside them with a loud slap, followed by two bags of frozen peas. Shannon jumped. She glared over Jimmy's shoulder.

"Terence, will you grow up?" she said. "I wouldn't have to do this if you hadn't thrown your damn coffee at him. Now go inside. Please."

"Maybe you'd like me to go into town," Terence said, "give you two some alone time? What do you need, Jimmy, an hour?"

Jimmy glanced at Shannon, at those long tanning bed legs of hers climbing out of the green Wellies.

"Mmm, better make it three," he said over his shoulder.

Shannon stifled a laugh.

"You cunt," Terence said.

Terence slammed the door behind him. Shannon closed her eyes and took a breath. Then she folded the wet towel and laid it on Jimmy's cheek, while he held a bag of peas against his neck.

"Better?" she asked.

"Yeah."

From the front of the house there was the sound of a car engine roaring and fading down the hill. Terence's Shelby Cobra, sounded like. Shannon groaned.

"Thanks, Jimmy. He's going to be a pain in my ass for the next *month*. Christ. Just when I had that whole thing settled."

They were quiet for a few minutes holding the cold things on his face. A breeze came up, scattering the leaves away from the pool and banking them up against the pool house. Shannon lifted up the towel and bit her lower lip.

"Jesus, Jimmy, this is *not* good. You'd better get to a doctor. It's really red. I think it's going to blister."

"It doesn't matter."

"Doesn't matter?" she said. "You're going to look like a freak if you don't treat this."

"I'll be fine." He forced a smile. "Maybe I'll sue your husband. Tell him I'll settle for the cost of Crystal's college."

She reapplied the towel to his cheek. "Something's going on. You're here and we're alone, so you might as well tell me."

"What makes you think that?"

"Please. Maybe the fact that you rode up here on a *horse* and you're dressed like Lord Greystoke."

"Greystoke?"

"Tarzan?" she said. "You know, when they take him back to England?"

"Right, the movie," Jimmy said. "Is that the one with Bo Derek?"

"No, you perv. Could you answer my question?"

"It's the only way I could see you," he said. "The Hunt. I wanted a chance for us to talk."

"*Talk*, huh? Well, we're not starting all *that* up again," she said, and by the weight she put on the word "that," Jimmy knew exactly what she was referring to: their afternoons at the Red Pony when she was supposedly volunteering at the retirement home, their weekends at the St. Regis in Manhattan, and their morning quickies in her SUV parked on the fire tower access road.

"Relax," he said. "I couldn't even if I wanted to. I don't have the time anymore. The towel. Move it, please."

She did, and he replaced it with the other bag of peas.

"I wish you'd go to the emergency room," she said. "Or I could call Dr. Hale, have him come over here."

"Shannon, I should have treated you better," Jimmy said.

"What are you talking about?"

He shrugged. "Like maybe I should have been with you exclusively."

"What?" She leaned away from him. "Oh, Jimmy..." She folded the towel and placed it on the end of the chaise. "You mean like a *boyfriend?* As in *going steady?* Are you serious?"

Shannon stood and went to the patio table a few feet away. She brushed the leaves off a chair, sat down and crossed her legs. For some reason, the green rubber boots made her stellar stems seem even longer.

"Jimmy? I'm up here."

He looked up. Shannon was facing him with her elbow on her knee and her palm under her chin. It was the most serious he'd ever seen her.

"I never cared about the other women," she said. "No offense, but I was only with you for one reason, and it *wasn't* emotional support."

"Okay."

"Oh, you're hurt." She smiled. "Please, Jimmy, face it—you were never 'settling down' material." She thought for a second and snapped her fingers. "Ah, this is good. I read this great biography of Alice Roosevelt the other day—what a spitfire, Jimmy, you would have liked her— and I never knew this, but her family was trying to get her to marry her cousin, Franklin—you know, F.D.R.? Anyway, guess what she said? She said the reason she wouldn't marry him was that he was the kind of boy that, quote, 'one invited to the dance, but not to dinner,' unquote."

"Unquote." He grinned and shook his head. "I always liked that brain of yours."

She buffed her nails on her shirt and mock-examined them at arm's length. "I'm not *summa cum laude* from Stanford for nothing. But do you get what I'm trying to say?"

The faint barking of hounds wafted up the hill with the breeze, the sound competing with the honking of southbound geese overhead. That smell of burning leaves was back, too.

"Who's burning leaves?" he asked. "Your gardener?"

She sat up straight and sniffed.

"I don't smell any leaves burning," she said. "It's... nothing, actually." Shannon stood and held out a hand for him. "You should get going. If you're still here when Terence gets back, he's going to think we *were* screwing."

"Yeah," Jimmy said.

"Take the peas," she said, helping him up. "And you know what I meant about F.D.R., right?"

"Sure. You don't want to feed me."

"Yes, that's exactly what I meant." She rolled her eyes.

"Goodbye, Shannon."

"Goodbye, Jimmy."

They shook hands, and she went into the house. Still holding the peas to his face, he turned and walked up the hill without looking back.

On his way to the Hammersley estate, Jimmy had to hide with the horse beneath a bridge across Wellington Creek while the hunters, horses and hounds galumphed past overhead. He felt like Josey Wales in the Clint Eastwood movie. When it was clear again, he led the horse onto a bridle path through the woods, heading east. If he was reading the map correctly, the Hammersley place was a mile or two away.

It was 12:29 and he'd met with only two of the six women on his list. Already his thighs ached and his tail-bone throbbed. With just five hours of solid daylight left, he needed to shorten his visits or skip some of the women. Jimmy touched his neck and cheek where the coffee had burned him. He could feel the give of his skin along his lower jaw. Blisters were starting to form. Great. His cheek stung, but it was nothing like the brittle pain he felt on his neck every time his head swayed in the saddle. The burn seemed to have awakened his other pains, too—especially the one through his abdomen and chest that felt like an expanding, spiked tube, unpredictably sending shooting pains through him if he moved the wrong way.

The fact was, he'd waited too long. He first sensed that something was wrong a year and a half ago, when he felt a sharp pain in his side. The pain persisted, but Jimmy thought he'd simply pulled a muscle. Then he awoke one morning and it was gone, and he forgot about it until it came back—this time a little higher in his torso. Fatigue and nausea followed. He decided he was working too hard, took a vacation to Key West, and once again the pain disappeared. When it returned a few weeks later, it was almost intolerable, and the weird thing was, even then, without having gone to the doctor yet, he knew what it was, yet he still did nothing about it. He didn't want to see doctors, hoping instead that whatever it was would just *go away*. He'd known other men, strong men, including his uncle, who were reduced to hairless, impotent fractions of themselves from chemo and radiation. Jimmy had decided that he'd rather live a shorter, more satisfying life than a protracted, miserable one.

To try to make up for all his debauchery, Jimmy had been spending more time with Crystal. During their visitations lately, Jimmy didn't waste time playing video games with her; they had a couple of beers and he talked to her like she was an adult. He told her about sex and instructed her to avoid guys like him. While her father had his good qualities, he told her—like honesty in business and pride in his work—he had been a complete shit toward women, including Crystal's mom.

While Jimmy was daydreaming, the horse had led them through the woods into a broad field. There was no fence around the field, and the grass was high and uncut. There was a road a few hundred yards away. A couple cars passed by. This field looked familiar; he was pretty sure this was the edge of the Hammersley estate.

He still had no idea what he would say to Natasha, but he had faith that this time the right words would come. He wagged the reins and trotted into the grass.

A hundred yards into the field, the ground rose, crested and began a gradual slide down to a dell. And there was the red- and white-striped balloon—the one that had been losing altitude earlier when he was at Shannon's. The half-deflated balloon was hanging from an oak tree on the edge of the field with the basket suspended 20 feet off the ground. As he got closer with the horse, he noticed two people in the basket: the pilot in a leather jacket and Yankees cap, and a brown-haired woman in a fur coat. The woman waved to him.

"Hello, hello there? You. Is that you, John?"

Jimmy trotted toward the beached balloon until he was underneath the basket. The woman looked over the basket edge and smiled with relief. It was Caterina Orlando.

"James?"

"Yes, it's me."

"Thank God! I've been stuck up here for an hour."

The pilot leaned over the edge. "I've called my crew. I have no idea what's taking them." He scanned the field. "Did you see anybody? They'll be on ATVs."

"Nobody," Jimmy said.

"James," Caterina said, slapping the side of the basket, "I'm coming down."

"Mrs. Orlando, please don't," the pilot said. "If you fall, you could break your legs."

She took off her mink coat. "Here, James, catch!"

The mink coat flying down looked like an enormous vampire bat. Jimmy almost fell out of the saddle reaching for it, but he grabbed it before it hit the ground.

"Good catch, darling," Caterina said. "Coming down."

"Mrs. Orlando," the pilot said, "I'm not insured for this."

A thick rope plummeted to the leaves, and not five seconds later Caterina was over the side, clutching the rope wearing a pair of kid gloves. Where she got the gloves, Jimmy had no idea. Once she had the rope entwined around her legs and between her thighs, she lowered herself hand-under-hand with such steadiness and precision, Jimmy would have sworn she'd had military training. There was much about Cat that he didn't know. The sight of the ever-elegant Caterina Orlando doing something as prosaic as climbing down a rope was mesmerizing.

When she reached the ground (without so much as breathing heavily), Jimmy got his first good look at her in over a year. She wore a chocolate jumpsuit with a plunging neckline that showed the tops of her breasts. A belt with a gold buckle was cinched smartly at the waist. Jimmy handed her the mink, and as she slipped it on she said, "James, I need a ride to Natasha's."

"Fine," he said.

He had her stand on a large rock and rode over for her to climb aboard. She straddled the horse, wrapped her arms around him, and they were on their way. At the bottom of the dell, he found a path worn with tire tracks. He followed it. Caterina spoke over his shoulder.

"I suppose you think you're my shining knight," she said. "Oh, James...your neck...what happened?"

"A burn. Accident."

"I didn't know you were part of the Hunt. Or are you a renegade?"

"Neither. It's a disguise."

The pain from his insides was making him sweat beneath his coat. He unbuttoned it. Caterina's gloved hands slid down past his waist until she was holding on to his parted inner thighs.

"Cat," he said, "I'm trying to concentrate."

She laughed. Her hands slithered back to his waist.

"So, how have you been, James?"

Before he had a chance to answer, the path emerged from the woods, and Jimmy took in a surreal sight: at least two dozen patio tables with white umbrellas, sitting in the middle of a recently mown, emerald meadow. Riding past, he saw the formal place settings on each table, the wait staff sitting on the sidelines smoking, and the people in chef's hats behind a row of grills. The smell of charcoal was pungent. If he was going to apologize to Caterina, now was the time.

"Listen, Cat, there's something—"

"Over there." She pointed. "That's the horse tent."

Jimmy rode to the tent, where a pair of men helped Caterina and him down and took the horse inside.

"Thank you, James. I see you soon, I hope." She kissed him on the cheek and headed for the bar. Jimmy winced at a fresh twinge of pain, and when he noticed one of the grooms watching him, he erupted.

"What are you looking at?"

"I'm sorry, sir," he said.

"Where is Mrs. Hammersley?" Jimmy asked.

"Here she comes, sir."

He pointed at a woman in hunting attire walking carefully across the meadow. It was Natasha's daughter, Titania.

"Not *Miss* Hammersley," Jimmy said to the groom. "*Missizz*—Natasha."

"Yes, of course." The groom wore one of those short-brimmed caps like Irish hoodlums used to wear, and he adjusted it on his head. "Over there, sir. She's the one in the top hat."

"What about *Mister* Hammersley?" Jimmy asked.

"He's on the Hunt, sir." The groom smirked as he walked away.

Even though it was still cool out, Jimmy was sweating and queasy. Lightheaded. He wanted to sit down, but it was more important to him to see Natasha. He did *not* want to be here when John Hammersley returned, even though Jimmy was fairly sure the guy had no idea about Jimmy and his wife.

He walked into the meadow and saw her: standing beside a caterer's truck, pointing around the picnic site with a riding crop. Her top hat had black netting dangling from the front, her hair was up, and she wore an old-fashioned woman's riding habit—the type of dress women used to wear to ride sidesaddle. The collar and cuffs were trimmed with white lace. Jimmy admired her profile. Of all the women he'd bedded, Natasha was the most aristocratic-looking, which was ironic, since she came from dire poverty in Russia.

Natasha turned in Jimmy's direction, and when he smiled at her, her face became stone. She walked to the horse tent, spoke with the grooms and exited from the back, where she got into a Range Rover and drove toward the house.

Jimmy decided to follow her. He had made it to the path and begun walking when five grooms—two of them enormous men—came out of the horse tent. One of them was holding Jimmy's horse by the bridle.

"'Scuse me, sir," he said, "but Mrs. Hammersley says you're to leave. She said that if you try to stay, we're to eject you from the premises."

The men surrounded him.

"So much for Hunt hospitality," Jimmy said.

"You need to ride on," said the burliest one—a guy who looked like all he'd ever done in his life was toss hay bales.

The groom handed him the reins and crouched to give him a boost.

"I can do it myself," Jimmy said.

He had to hop a couple of times to do it, and when he finally thrust himself up onto the saddle he was light-headed and sweating from the pain, but he managed on his own and rode down the path he'd come in on. Once he was out of view, Jimmy turned into the trees and rode around the meadow through the woods. The grooms had returned to work, and as soon as he was clear of them, he rode out to the path and cantered up to the mansion.

Of all of the hilltoppers' residences, the Hammersleys' looked the most like an English manor, which is exactly what the Robber Baron-rich, vain and unimaginative John Hammersley had intended. Built of sandstone and granite, the original structure dated back to the early 1800s. When Hammersley doubled the size of the place five years ago, Jimmy had been the general contractor on the project. Jimmy knew the house well.

Not wanting to embarrass Natasha, he tied up the horse behind the box hedge maze and crept into the rhododendrons that grew along the mansion's back windows. The ground floor windows on the entire mansion were tall ground-to-ceiling ones, and John Hammersley kept one of them unlocked: the one to his billiard room. He kept it unlocked to give himself the ability to slip out at night unnoticed, meet his mistress in her car at the foot of the driveway, and return a few hours later. Jimmy liked the irony: that the same window John kept unlocked for his own adulterous purposes had been used by Jimmy for *his* adulterous purposes with Natasha.

As usual, the window was unlocked. Once inside, he went to the door and listened. There was the woody echo of boots on the marble floor, and then Natasha said, "I go to lie down. Please call me when the hunters arrive."

Jimmy heard her go upstairs. He waited, then went out in the hall and dashed up there himself. He went in her bedroom and closed the door silently behind him. Natasha's top hat was at the foot of the bed. The sink was running in the bathroom. Jimmy sat on the bed, trying not to move too much so he wouldn't aggravate the sharp pain through his middle. His neck stung like a bitch, too.

Then the bathroom door opened and she breezed into the bedroom, her posture exquisite as usual. She glanced at the bed, saw him, and stopped short.

"Jimmy, I said for you to leave. I have a hundred guests today. You should not be here."

He patted the bedspread beside him. "Sit down. Please."

She crossed her arms, exposing the white lace cuffs of her blouse.

"You look beautiful in that outfit, by the way," he said. "Like a princess. A Russian princess."

Her mouth twitched into a smile and fell again, but he knew then that she would join him.

"Come on, Tash. I just want to talk."

"Yes," she said, "I heard about your little journey today. Apologizing to all of your *women*."

"Sit down, please. For a minute."

She cast those exotic eyes of hers away from him and stared at the rug for what seemed like minutes. Then, with a huff, she smoothed her skirt under her legs and eased onto the bed about a foot away from him. Although a decade older than he, Natasha was prettier than most women half her age. She crossed her arms and stared across the room at the nude painting of herself by local artist Dwight Anderson. Jimmy glanced at the painting and turned back to her.

Unlike other women, whose faces pinched up and revealed every flaw and wrinkle when they were sad or angry, Natasha's became taut and petulant, and the slight protrusion of her lips was especially attractive. To him, her face was more than striking; it was hauntingly beautiful.

"I listen," she said. "So go on, *talk*. Apologize."

"Tash, I—"

"And do not call me 'Tash.'"

"Come on, my little Russkie."

This time she smiled and it held. She scanned his face, then reached out and gently touched his neck and cheek.

"I heard what Terence did," she said.

"It's not that bad."

She ran her hand down his jacket. Her fingers were so slender, her nails the perfect length. Hardly the hands of a woman who had been born into poverty.

"I have missed you, Jimmy," she said. "You make me laugh. With you, I never pretend. You don't mind hearing about my life in Russia, before I become rich Mrs. Hammersley. This is why I am so angry when you leave. You *abandon* me." She thumped her fists on her thighs.

Jimmy scooted next to her and kissed her. There had always been something electric in her lips, as though she were brimming over with life force, and by kissing her he could draw off some of it for himself. Her cheeks were cool. He tipped her back in his arms onto the bed, where they kissed and caressed each other. Kissing a woman had never felt so natural. Today, for the first time ever, he was content to kiss her, and nothing else.

Then she began to greedily unbutton his hunting jacket, and he did something he'd never done before: he sprang up in the bed and pushed her away. The force of his sudden realization made his eyes well up.

"Jimmy?" she said.

"I loved you, Tash. And I still do."

She gaped at him.

"That's why I had to dump you," he said. "It seemed impossible. Hell, it *is* impossible."

Natasha shifted on the bed to face him. She clutched his hands. "But why have you never told me this?"

"I didn't know. Not until a second ago, kissing you."

The bedside telephone rang. It was one of those ornate gold phones with an actual bell. Natasha answered it.

"Yes?" She smiled wearily at him. "Tell them I come down in ten minutes." She hung up and steadied herself on the nightstand. Her back was to him. "My luncheon. The hunters are on their way."

"Go," Jimmy said. "Enjoy your party."

"I am sorry I cannot let you stay, but you know why," she said. "Tonight, late. I come to your house. We talk about this."

She stood, donned her top hat and checked herself in the mirror. Jimmy got off the bed slowly, wincing at the pain in his abdomen, and wrapped his arms around her.

"God, you're gorgeous."

"Later." She peeled his arms off and went to the door. "And do not let yourself be seen. I will wave when it is clear."

He lagged behind in the doorway while she went to the stairs. He checked his phone: 2:04. Once Natasha waved to him, he quickstepped to the landing and went down the stairs. At the bannister, he lifted her veil and kissed her one more time. Already he felt a surge of energy and a distance from his worries; it was the closest thing to happiness that he'd experienced in months.

"Later, Tash?"

"Yes, later."

———— ·•◆•· ————

By three o'clock, Jimmy was miles from the Hammersley estate, but he still had two women to see (three, if he counted Crystal's mother) and besides being in great pain, he was running out of energy, not to mention daylight. He had consulted the map again, pinpointed Gillian Barnes's place, and sallied forth along a creek, past Wellington Lake, and across a Rabbitsville boarding farm. Twenty years earlier, Jimmy had seen a tornado cut a swath through the woods here. Now, although the sun was getting lower in the sky, it was still clear and bright. But as he climbed a treeless hilltop, he made out a wall of steel-blue clouds, stretched low on the western horizon. The first of the autumn storms was coming. Probably tomorrow.

He rode the length of a cornfield between the tree line and the unharvested corn, its gray-yellow stalks high and full and rustling in the wind. The cornfield abutted Route 33 on one end, and as soon as Jimmy saw the old one-room schoolhouse—now a historic landmark—he realized he was wasn't far from the Wellington Country Store, where he could get some water and maybe treat his burn. Jimmy steered the horse onto the wide, grassy shoulder and set out at a trot.

He passed a favorite watering hole for locals like him—The Top of the Stretch—passed Samantha Cutler's farm stand (where he had once vigorously taken Sammy bent over a bushel of eggplants), and passed the aging Wellington Lanes before he reached the store. It was a blue cedar-shake Cape with three ugly additions—none of which Jimmy had been contracted to build—and the poor workmanship showed, including rotting soffits and a sagging roof.

Since the store catered to the horsey set, there were long hitching rails on the sides of the parking lot. He got down and tied the horse off. He wasn't looking forward to going inside. The now-owner, Brigitte Archambault—daughter of snooty French-Canadian bakers—had been the only girl in high school to turn him down for a date.

He went inside. Brigitte's daughter, Marie, greeted him. Jimmy liked her; of all of Crystal's friends, Marie was by far the sharpest.

"Hi, Jimmy," she said.

Behind her, Brigitte was rolling dough.

"*Marie*," she said.

"Sorry," Marie said. "Hey, *Mister Tatko*. I was just texting with your daughter, *Crystal*. How are you this afternoon, *sir*?"

Jimmy turned his burned face and neck away from them. "Very good, Marie, thanks."

"Marie," Brigitte said, untying her apron. "I have to go to Bendini's for parchment paper. Watch the store."

"Yes, Mom."

Brigitte put on a coat, grabbed her purse and left without a word to Jimmy. As soon as she was gone, Marie looked at Jimmy's neck and pressed her fingers against her own.

"Ouch. What's this?"

"Little burn," he said. "No problem."

"I didn't know you were part of the Hunt."

Jimmy got a bottle of water from the cooler and some burn cream on a shelf.

"Yeah. Listen, can I use your bathroom?"

"Go ahead."

He went in. A few minutes later, when he opened the door again, Marie was there. Her face was grim.

"You've got to get out of here. They're calling the police!"

Jimmy heard men and women jabbering on the other end of the store.

"What?" he said. "Who?"

Marie put a finger to her lips and tugged him out of the bathroom. The two of them peeked around the corner. A dozen scarlet jackets were crowded around the front counter. Marie whispered to him.

"They're saying that's one of Mr. Highgate's horses outside, and that you stole it. Did you?"

"Of course not," Jimmy said. "I have permission."

"I told them it's been there since this morning." She frowned. "My mother'll be pissed when she finds out. You know she doesn't like you, right?"

"Believe me, I know," Jimmy said.

"You need to get out of here."

She led him by the arm through a storeroom and opened the back door.

"No one's watching the horse, I checked," Marie said. "Be careful, Jimmy."

"Thanks, Marie."

He walked the horse down the path behind the store, and as soon as he was out of sight, he looped around the building, crossed the road, and trotted up the hill behind the bowling alley. At the top of the hill, he stopped and looked back at the store parking lot. The village police cruiser pulled in. It was time to go.

Steering the horse into the trees, he ducked under a limb and saw a paper coffee cup sitting in the fallen leaves. A sobering thought occurred to him: he would be dead before that cup decomposed.

———————————————

When he reached the hilltop where Gillian Barnes and Leah Gold were neighbors, the steel-blue clouds gathering to the west magically parted, washing the entire expanse of grass and colorful trees in warm sun, as though Gillian, the billionaire widow, had paid for one final afternoon of Indian summer. Now it was hot. Jimmy took off his coat.

At Gillian's house, the Asian housekeeper—Jimmy could never remember the woman's name—said Gillian was next door at Ms. Gold's, playing tennis. She shut the door in his face. Jimmy walked over to Leah's.

On his way down the stairs to the tennis court, Jimmy could hear the sucking and popping sounds of a ball machine, followed by the twang of a racquet. When he reached the fence gate, Jimmy paused outside. Leah was on the court. She hit a strong two-handed backhand down the line, where it disappeared into a pile of leaves against the fence. A young man—a strapping blonde kid; he couldn't have been older than 20 or 21—stood against the fence with a ball basket, while another—his *twin?*—stood a few yards away with another basket. At the next ball, Leah took a few chirping steps to her right and hit a forehand shot crosscourt. Her ponytail bounced on her shoulders, and her baby-blue tennis dress stretched deliciously tight on her backside.

Jimmy went in with the fence gate squeaking and clanking shut behind him. Gillian, whom he hadn't noticed, leaned forward out of the umbrellaed shade of the umpire chair. She had a glass of rosé in her hand.

"Well, well," Gillian said, peering at him from across the court. "Look what we have here. If it isn't the great Jimmy Tatko." She climbed down from the umpire chair holding her wine glass.

"What?" Leah let the next ball bounce past her. "Shut it off, Tommy, will you?" She tapped the racquet against her leg. "And boys? Take a walk. You can pick up the balls later."

"Okay, Leah," Tommy said.

The twins exited the gate. As their footsteps faded up the stairs, Jimmy pointed over his shoulder with his thumb.

"They keep getting younger and younger, ladies."

"Sit down, Jimmy." Gillian waved at some chairs on the sidelines. The three of them sat down. "I heard about your little odyssey today. Your *mission*."

"Who told you?" he asked.

"It doesn't matter. I'll save you some time, though. You don't owe *me* any apologies, but you owe Leah here a big one. And by 'big one,' I mean an apology, not something else you might want to give her. So, go on. Apologize."

"Would you like something to drink, Jimmy?" Leah reached into a cooler at her feet.

"No, I'm fine."

Gillian's stare on him was withering; Leah, meanwhile, couldn't look him in the eyes.

"We're waiting, Jimmy," Gillian said.

The same sense of clarity he'd experienced when he woke up that morning washed over him again, but it wasn't solely Gillian's taunts that triggered it. It was the hot splash of sun on the tennis court, surrounded by explosive foliage and dark clouds in the distance. It was the burn on his neck, the strangling pain he felt inside, and the ridiculous riding clothes he wore. It was the miles and miles he'd ridden that day, the women he'd seen, and the lack of closure he felt. All of these combined to give him this moment of clarity, and he realized, with a shiver of fear, how little time he had left.

It could be weeks, or days, or even *hours*, so why was he wasting them by apologizing for how he'd lived? The fact was, most of the women he'd been involved with over the years had actively discouraged him from improving himself, because they'd wanted him—or *part* of him any-way—for their own selfish needs. Natasha and Victoria were the only ones who ever truly cared about him. An urge to see Natasha, to hold her and hear that adorable accent of hers, came upon him so swiftly that he felt his nose tingle and his eyes begin to water, and before he realized what he was doing, he was out of his chair and walking toward the gate.

"What the *fuck*, Jimmy!" Gillian said.

He was going to ignore her, but something in her voice irked him, and he had to say something. The words, the words that had been bottled up inside him all day long, now poured out.

"Gillian," he said, "we both know why I don't owe you an apology. As for you, Leah—you knew what I was about before we got involved. Nobody forced you. You were bored and you wanted the drama, and you knew that good old Jimmy could provide it. Neither of you ever encouraged me to be a better man. You wanted me exactly the way I was. And if those two boys I just saw tell me anything, you two haven't changed and probably never will. So, you know what? To hell with both of you. I've wasted enough time. Goodbye."

He walked out, leaving the gate open behind him. He climbed the stairs. The twins were sitting on the brickwork at the top.

"Guys," Jimmy said, "I don't care how much they're paying you, it's not worth it. Go be with a couple girls your own age."

They stared at him without saying anything, their blonde eyebrows crinkling up in unison. Jimmy sighed, crossed Leah's dormant rose garden, climbed wearily aboard the horse one last time and cantered west, toward the Highgate estate.

———◆———

Back home, he grabbed two beers from the refrigerator, stripped and drank one of them in the shower. He didn't know what to make of the day. He felt a lonely satisfaction about what he'd done, like he'd run a marathon and no one else would ever know about it. Even though he wasn't much of a horseback rider, he'd enjoyed seeing a lot of the Wellington countryside that he loved so much.

Stepping out of the shower, Jimmy toweled off and opened the second beer. He walked into the bedroom, switched on the light and saw a golf club on the rug, along with shards of glass. The window closest to the road was shattered.

Carmel. It had to be her.

He put on his work boots in the other room, and wearing nothing but the towel vacuumed up the glass with the Shop-Vac. After he threw out the big shards, he changed into comfortable clothes, went outside and patched the window by nailing a sheet of plywood over the entire window frame.

It was nine o'clock by the time he finished, and although physically exhausted he was alert and would be ready for her when she arrived. He lit the pre-made fire in the fireplace, pulled the bottle of Grey Goose from the freezer and set it on the counter with a highball glass. Then he lay on the couch and watched the fire. The pain, the pain that had accompanied him all day long, was gone again, and his eyes were heavy. He wanted to sleep. More than anything he wanted to sleep.

But not until Natasha got here.

9

GARBAGE FEUD

It all started when my wife and I were moving a mile out of the village and we needed to throw out a few bags of trash. Crawford had a 30-yard Dumpster across the street with plenty of room in it, and I had the permission of one of his tenants. Or so I thought.

Our first morning in the new apartment, I got a call from that tenant: my artist friend Dwight Anderson. I'd never heard him so nervous before.

"Listen," he said, "this may be superfluous, but do you recall the trash you threw in Crawford's Dumpster yesterday?"

"Yeah?"

"Well, I bumped into him back there a few minutes ago, and he's opening bags. He asked me if I'd seen anything. I played coy."

"I don't understand," I said. "Why didn't you tell him you gave me permission?"

"Oh, I couldn't do that. I told you—I can't get involved."

"You also told me it was okay."

"No, I *said* that I didn't see how it would be a problem."

"Well, the distinction would have been nice to know, Dwight—*before* I threw the stuff out."

"Nevertheless, my situation with Crawford is tenuous, and I can't afford to be party to any theft of service."

"*Theft of service?*"

"Yes. You used a service—his trash removal—without compensating him. The law would consider it theft of service. Possibly civil trespass to boot. It wouldn't surprise me if he called the police."

"I thought I threw some trash in my friend's Dumpster," I said. "It didn't seem sinister."

"It never does."

I hesitated before replying. For years Dwight had shown me his nudes of hot Wellington trophy wives when the paintings were still works in progress, and I was loath to lose the privilege. But this wasn't the first time he had pulled a stunt like this, and I was sick of it.

"You know what, Dwight?" I said. "Don't call me anymore."

All that first week in the new apartment, through chinks in the blinds I caught glimpses of Crawford's truck marauding the streets. He drove a retired Entenmann's delivery truck that had been hastily repainted before being put into service for his contracting company. Still showing through the thin coat of white on the sides were the navy blue Entenmann's logo, a 6-foot pecan danish ring and the tagline *"Simply Irresistible."* When the truck accelerated, its engine rattled, shaking the buildings on the street, as though the vehicle itself were overcompensating for an inferiority complex: a former pastry truck thrown into the macho world of general contracting.

For days I rationalized my not going outside because it was oppressively hot and humid. Thunderstorms threatened as the week went on, and when my wife brought up the subject of our security deposit on the old apartment, I used the weather as an excuse for not going into town.

"I can't ride my bike in a thunderstorm," I said.

"Oh, for God's sake," she said, "take an umbrella and walk. We *need* that money. Mr. Nickerson is a cheap old coot, and I don't trust him to mail it to us. The only way we're getting that money back is by you going in and prying it out of his fingers."

On the eighth day, the weather cleared and I had no more excuses. Suddenly I was faced with an unpleasant truth about myself: I was afraid to go out.

Dwight's mention of police and "theft of service" had whipped me into a panic. I cooked my brain trying to remember exactly what we had thrown out in Crawford's Dumpster, and the more I thought about it, the less I could be sure we hadn't disposed of something incriminating. I paced the living room. In our haste, had we included old bills in the household trash? Was there *anything* with our names on it?

Outside, a truck roared by. I peered out the blinds. It was a moving truck.

Crap. The labels on the moving boxes. They were fluorescent yellow with room names and contents written on them. We'd also used the same paper for a "RETURN" label taped to the garbage can on our old front lawn. The trash company was supposed to have picked up the can by now, but on the off-chance they hadn't, I needed to get that label.

Technically our new apartment was only a mile from the village, but the road we lived on was one Crawford had been patrolling. So, I took a more circuitous route—five miles long, over dirt roads, through the woods.

The first half was a blistering uphill grind, but at the top of Chestnut Ridge the road became downhill all the way to the village. It was a series of steep dips and switchbacks, not for inexperienced cyclists or drivers whose brakes needed servicing.

I coasted. The wind washed over my face, the hazy sunlight beamed through holes in the canopy, and for the first time in over a month, I felt something close to serenity.

My favorite part of the ride was the long downhill straightaway after the switchbacks. A house abutted the road, and along the shoulder the weekender who owned the property had placed a series of signs, like the old "Burma Shave" signs. Every time I rode by here, the signs made me smile.

OLD DOG

YOUNG DOG

SEVERAL STUPID DOGS

SO PLEASE DON'T FROWN

JUST <u>SLOW DOWN</u>

AND LET OUR DOGS BE STUPID

I coasted the rest of the way into the village, and when I reached the paved streets I kept an eye out for white trucks.

I dashed into the post office and mailed the bills, then stood outside the liquor store, gazing at a window display for Maker's Mark Kentucky Straight Bourbon, and biting my lower lip. No. I had to go over to the old apartment. Get the garbage can label and our security deposit and go home.

Turning onto my old street, I saw the feed store and remembered that my cat was out of her exotic dry food. Unfortunately this was the only place I could get it, and Crawford owned the store. His truck wasn't around, but I was still making this quick. I leaned my bike against a stack of fertilizer beneath the overhang and walked through the open bay doors.

The big open room smelled of sweet grain. As my eyes adjusted to the dimness, I made out a tanned, yellow-haired beauty at the counter, cupping her chin in one hand, flipping through a magazine with the other. It was Crawford's daughter. Mid-20s, slim and incongruently stacked, she possessed such rare beauty—the kind of heart-stopping pulchritude that inspires poets to write or whack off—that I couldn't believe she was the offspring of such a miserable prick. Luckily she didn't know me. I took off my bike helmet and tousled my hair.

"Pretty hot, huh?"

She wore a black tank top with black bra straps showing on her soft shoulders.

"Yeah. Help you find anything?"

"Cat food. The 'Katz-n-Flocken' stuff."

"Over there, purple bag."

I fetched one. On my way back to the register, a pair of silver-haired men in Hunter Wellies—those $500 rubber boots designed for Noah-sized floods—sauntered in unison into the store. I nodded at their boots.

"Expecting a typhoon, gentlemen?"

They pretended not to hear me. It was this kind of pretentiousness that made me embarrassed to be from Wellington. The douchebags wore Wellies even during the deepest droughts, like this summer. At the counter I handed Crawford's daughter my credit card. She looked at it and said, "Hey, you're the guy that lives across the street."

"No, afraid not."

She scowled. And let me tell you, on a gorgeous woman's face, a scowl is particularly unpleasant.

"Yes you are," she said. "My father's been looking for you. That was horrible what you did, throwing out all that trash."

"What are you talking about?"

"*Please,*" she said. "He found an Amazon receipt with your name on it."

"Whatever. Ring up the cat food and I'll leave."

"No. I'm not selling it to you." She tossed my credit card on the counter. I put it in my wallet.

"Okay," I said.

We both lunged for the bag, but I got it first.

"Hey!" she said.

As I stuffed the cat food in my knapsack, the two silver-hairs walked over.

"Is there a problem here?" one of them said.

"Get lost, Wellies."

I fished out some bills and slapped them down. She pulled a phone out of her shorts pockets and started typing.

"I'm telling my father."

"Tell him I said hello."

I marched out, got on the bike and pedaled up the street, toward my old apartment.

All of the parking places on the street were occupied by pickup trucks, and there were even a couple of trucks double-parked. I couldn't tell what was happening yet, but the lawn in front of my house bustled with activity. As I got closer, I noticed that the garbage can was still at the curb, but the yellow label was gone and the can looked full.

It couldn't be; they picked up our trash days ago.

I parked my bike under the shade tree between my house and Mr. Nickerson's. Close to a dozen men were rummaging through big plastic bins on my lawn. They were showing each other what looked like magazines and laughing. On my way over to them, I checked out the garbage can: it brimmed with broken drywall, wood and shingle scraps.

"Hey, what's going on?" I asked the men.

"You live here?" one of them said.

"Used to."

"Jesus, this is one huge friggen collection you got."

"Yeah," said another. "When did you *sleep?*"

They laughed.

"What are you talking about?" I said.

Taped to one of the bins was a sheet of paper with "FREE" scrawled across it. Inside the bins were stacks of porn magazines, videocassettes and DVDs. I counted the bins. Seven heavy-duty storage bins, packed with porn. The contracting waste in the garbage can told me that this was all Crawford's doing.

"This stuff isn't mine," I said.

"Sure, sure. You know, you probably should of E-Bayed some. Especially the vintage stuff. You got magazines here from the sixties, dude."

"I'm telling you, they're not mine," I said. "I wasn't even *born* in the sixties."

The men scrutinized each magazine and video, tossing back the ones they didn't want. They all held sizable armloads of the stuff.

"Hey," I said, "why don't you just take it all? You've got trucks."

"Nah."

Mr. Nickerson came over from next door, walking his deaf and mostly blind terrier. He frowned at me.

"This filth, is it yours?"

"I have no idea whose it is, Mr. Nickerson. Somebody left it here."

The men snickered.

"Guys, could you leave now?" I said.

They grabbed some last-second items and shuffled away to their trucks comparing their finds.

"Stuff's been here since last night," Mr. Nickerson said. "Shouldn't of left the can here. Attracts the vagrants and everybody else to throw out their trash."

In Mr. Nickerson's universe, there were hordes of people driving around with car trunks full of garbage, hunting for decent citizens' cans to throw it in.

"I'm sorry, Mr. Nickerson, but the can should have been picked up by now. I came by to get our security deposit."

He wore a Cabot Cheese baseball cap. He took it off, smoothed his thinning hair, and yanked it back on.

"Well, I can't give you your security until this filth's out of here."

"Yes, Mr. Nickerson." I ripped down the "FREE" sign, picked up the loose trash on the lawn and shoved it in the bins.

"Boy," he said, "wouldn't I like to find the guy that did this. Like to dump the stuff on *his* lawn, see how he likes it."

He and the dog tottered down the sidewalk. When they were gone, I sat down on my old stoop, picked at the peeling paint and stared at the garbage. Maybe I could call the company and have them come back. Trouble was, I doubted they took contractor's waste. Or vats of porn.

There was a wealthy couple, the Wechslers, whose house I watched over when they were away, and at the moment they were in Africa. They had a pickup truck. I could borrow it to take this stuff to the dump.

Well, lesson learned: Never again would I try to use someone else's trash.

The neighbor's tabby, Huckleberry, was stretched out in the shade by the curb. He sat bolt upright and pricked up his ears, then trotted across the road to his owner's house, where he leapt into a porch swing and lay down facing me like a Sphinx.

Crawford's truck drifted around the corner, its engine rattling. Every muscle in my body tensed. As the truck crept past, Crawford stared at me. I nodded.

Hey, no hard feelings.

If only Crawford had responded with a nod of his own—even a half-assed, two-finger wave with his hands on the steering wheel—some signal between men that said, "OK, we're even." If he had, things might have turned out differently, and you wouldn't have heard anything about us. But the stoic expression on his face said he was convinced of his moral superiority. He wasn't giving an inch. What he gave me instead was the finger. He stared at me for the whole five seconds it took to crawl by, his arm fully extended across the truck cab, giving me the finger the entire time, like he was pumping a death ray into me. And when he turned the corner at the end of the block and I couldn't see his face anymore, he stuck his arm out the driver's window and continued giving me the finger, until he disappeared behind the feed store.

Up to this point, I had been willing—eager, in fact—to put this incident behind me. Crawford was justified in dumping trash on my old lawn. Even the porn was forgivable; it had wit. But giving me the finger? That was uncalled for.

This, I imagined, was why feuds never ended. Each party to the feud has a certain amount of crow he's willing to eat, and provided the other doesn't force him to eat more than that amount, there will be no more retribution. One of the Hatfields or the McCoys probably once said, *"If'n he kills my cousin or even my brother, that's all right. I'm a gettin' tired of this feud anyhow. But if that bastard pisses on his dead body, it's back on!"*

And then one of them did exactly that, and the feud continued.

———————◆◆◆———————

As I biked over to the Wechslers' to borrow their pickup, glimmers of a plan flashed into my head. It was as though my unconscious mind had been plotting this revenge against Crawford from the beginning and I was powerless to stop it.

Sweaty from the long ride in the glaring sun, I went in the garage and opened the refrigerator. I'd hoped to find some iced tea or lemonade, but instead I faced a *wall* of beer: Bass Ale, Sam Adams Summer Ale, Newcastle Brown Ale, Stella Artois. My wife had stopped letting me drink ever since I had gotten drunk, turned into Mr. Hyde and chopped up our coffee table with a hatchet. After that, alcohol and hatchets disappeared from the house. Chalking it up to fate, I downed a Newcastle while basking in the cool from the open door.

Then I pulled out the entire 12-pack of Stella.

I sat in a lawn chair next to the recycle bins, drinking beers and tossing the empties. Around my third or fourth, I spied a shiny orange Husqvarna chainsaw on the workbench. Its teeth glistened with oil. I opened another beer, took a sip, licked my eyetooth. A pastiche of violent music and movie scenes roiled inside me: "Welcome to the Jungle" by Guns n' Roses, the climactic shootout in *Scarface*, the napalm scene from *Apocalypse Now*. I chugged the beer and slung the empty bottle in the garbage can. I stood up with the remains of the 12-pack, started for the door, and stopped.

With my free hand, I grabbed the chainsaw on my way out.

Part one of my plan required finding out where Crawford lived. At the diner, I inquired discreetly, but the most anyone knew was that the daughter still lived at home, not where *home* was, so I staked out the feed store until it closed and followed her. It turned out that Crawford's place was a couple of miles north of the village.

To kill time, I got myself a pepperoni and sausage pizza at Vinny's and ate it in the truck in the library parking lot. The library was closed, and the town cop wasn't on duty, so I was able to wash down the pizza with the beers. After the initial four or five, I had paced myself; I wanted to maintain a nice buzz without turning into Mr. Hyde. For what I had in mind, I would need at least a semblance of sobriety.

Once it was dark, I returned to the old apartment. With the mindless strength only retarded or intoxicated men have, I got the heaping garbage can and vats o' porn into the truck bed. I was driving to Crawford's when my wife called.

"Where are you?" she said. "It's almost midnight. What are you doing?"

"Nothing, just driving around."

"*Driving?* Whose car?"

"It's a truck," I said.

"What's going on? Did you get the security?"

"What? You're breaking up on me."

"Are you drinking?"

"I'll call you back in a few minutes." I ended the call.

The road was desolate when I reached Crawford's mailbox, which was mashed-in on one side from a past encounter with a baseball bat. In the field across the way, hip-high corn rustled in a light breeze. I backed partway up his drive, parked with the engine running, got in the truck bed, and shoved everything on the pavement.

Crawford's house was up a long hill. There were no lights on.

Well, Crawford old buddy, that was about to change.

I popped one of Mr. Wechsler's Led Zeppelin CDs into the truck stereo and cranked the volume. The martial wails of "Immigrant Song" rang out of the speakers. Swinging the chainsaw by the handle, I loped up the drive. A pair of white birches, each about as big around as my thigh, shone in the moonlight. At the trees, I pulled out my phone and snapped a photo of myself holding up the chainsaw, then I set the choke, yanked the starter cord, and the Husqvarna whined to life. I stepped up to the first birch and let the teeth slowly bite into the wood until I had a good groove started.

Then I floored it.

Up the hill, a light went on. I bore down harder, but not too hard because I didn't want the saw blade to jam, and made my first notch low on the tree trunk. Pivoting, I sunk the teeth into the other side of the tree, a few inches higher than the first notch. Wood chips sprayed on my legs and forearms. I kept cutting until the tree shuddered, then stepped away and savored the tangy bouquet of fumes and wood pulp as the first tree toppled across the driveway.

Up on the hill, more lights flashed on, but I didn't care. Between the alcohol, the heady smells and noises, and the trembling power I held in my hands, my brain was singing an aria; it wasn't listening to reason. Revving the saw, I stepped up to the second tree.

A pair of headlights careened down the dark drive. I squeezed the throttle. A glint flashed in my periphery, and Crawford's truck appeared in the moonlight. Then the chainsaw sputtered. Coughed. Died. I yanked it out of the saw-cut.

Crawford yelled out the truck window: "What the fuck is this?!"

The second tree made very little noise coming down—a low groan—but it fell much faster than the first one, accelerating exponentially once past vertical. Meanwhile, Crawford's truck rolled forward. The tree crashed onto the engine hood and slid off with a protracted shriek. Crawford tried to jump out but was tangled up in branches.

"You sonovabitch! I'll kill you for this!"

I gave him the finger, put the chainsaw in the pickup, and kept giving him the finger out the window as I roared away.

———◆———

To this day, I have no idea how I got home that night. I woke up in my bed the next morning with a hangover that felt like the Ebola virus. As punishment for my drinking, my wife didn't talk to me, which was fine with me since I was in no mood or condition to talk anyway.

The next three weeks were nerve-wracking because I didn't see Crawford once. Up to this point I'd been avoiding confrontation, but now I craved a showdown. I started carrying a Buck folding knife, and anytime I heard a truck coming, I reached in my pocket and touched it.

Maybe it was because I had trash on the brain, but whenever I was walking along the road I noticed all kinds of garbage in roadside ditches and hollows: air conditioners, carpet remnants, cinder blocks, car seats, broken toilets, refrigerators and bald tires. Seeing the stuff made me angry. How much of a crime was my throwing a couple of bags of trash in Crawford's Dumpster, when I could just as easily have pitched them in the woods like these schmucks?

Then, on the same day that it rained torrentially, I got a web design project. Like the drought that summer, web design work had been scarce, so I had to take the job. It was a website for a local architect who expected me to work out of his office in the village. Since my wife and I had only one car, I would have to commute by bicycle. I hadn't seen Crawford in over a month, but I wasn't about to start tempting fate by taking the direct route into town. I used the back roads.

The sun was shining that morning, the blanket of ferns on the forest floor billowy and lush. A flock of wild turkeys milled around the tree line. I relaxed and let myself enjoy the smells of loam and recent rain. A cicada began its shrill song, like a golf course sprinkler. But when it reached what should have been its crescendo, not only did the sound fail to taper off, but it grew louder and more shrill. I stopped the bike. The sound was coming from behind me somewhere, morphing into a screech. There were clanging noises, too, and then the unmistakable sound of branches snapping.

I shoved off again with the bike, and while I pumped up the hill, a familiar noise penetrated the woods: the rattle of Crawford's truck engine. The snaps of tree branches got closer. I reached a treeless section of the road, looked down the hill, and saw the treetops shaking. The shaking was advancing up the hill behind me.

Even though I couldn't see him yet, I knew T-Rex was coming.

I reached the top. Ordinarily I'd pause here to catch my breath. Not today. I still couldn't see the truck, but it was close enough now that I could hear the leaves sweeping the metal. My foot slipped and my groin landed on the crossbar. A wave of nausea coursed through me. Then, in the rear-view mirror, a white shape lurched into view and there was no longer any doubt: Crawford was barreling up behind me. My mouth dried up, tasted bitter.

Going into the first turn, I dragged my inside foot for balance. Crawford's engine grill ballooned in my mirror until I banked into the turn, where he had to slow down and I lost him temporarily. Through the remaining switchbacks, the pattern was the same: I gained ground on the turns; he gained on the straightaways. Each time, my lead shrank.

In the final turn before the long downhill, I peered off the road. Why not go down there, where Crawford couldn't follow? Why not? Because the ground pitched down at a 60-degree angle and was a minefield of rocks and huge trees, that's why not. My one chance was to pedal like mad and get to a side road or driveway before Crawford caught up to me. I hurtled past the signs:

OLD DOG
YOUNG DOG
SEVERAL STUPID DOGS
SO PLEASE DON'T FROWN
JUST <u>SLOW DOWN</u>
AND LET OUR DOGS BE STUPID

Crawford was a car length behind me now, blasting his horn. I had no choice. I started to swerve toward the sheer hillside and an animal streaked out of the woods from the other side of the road. A yellow dog. It barked and cut in front of me. I swerved the other way, but I pulled too hard and the front tire skidded. I flew over the handlebars and landed in the ditch.

Face down with the wind knocked out of me, I heard a frantic honking, Crawford yelling "SHIT!" then the snapping of small trees and the clanging rumble of what sounded like a derailed train—Crawford's truck turning over and over with tools banging around inside.

The sound continued for a good ten seconds. It grew fainter and seemed to stop, and then there was another bang, until finally it ceased. The woods were still again. I got unsteadily to my feet. The dog, confused yet pleased with itself, barked down the hill.

I staggered to the edge of the ravine. The truck had cut a swath through the woods so deep that from the road I couldn't see where it ended. Broken limbs, flattened saplings and leaf-stripped branches lay in its wake.

I have to admit, my first instinct was not to help Crawford. Then for some reason I remembered a TV commercial for the Church of Jesus Christ of Latter-day Saints, in which a parishioner cut off by a driver finds that same driver crashed up the road. He forgives the man and helps him. I didn't forgive Crawford, nor was I overcome with altruistic feeling for my fellow man, but I did think about how grateful Crawford might be if I rescued him. Surely he'd drop the garbage feud. On the other hand, if I didn't help, and he lived, the feud would continue indefinitely.

I started down the precipitous hillside, sweaty and shaking, clutching saplings like ropes, questioning my sanity for doing this. Crawford hated me, and the damn truck might blow up. If I saved him, though, I'd be a hero in town.

From the top, Crawford's truck seemed to have rolled clear to the village, but in fact it had traveled only a couple hundred feet before slamming into an unforgiving tulip tree. A massive sucker, 100 years old at least. The driver's side was caved in. The truck leaned against the tree, its right wheels suspended two feet off the ground. From the damage I knew Crawford was dead, but I wasn't taking any chances. I went to the driver's door.

"Crawford?" I pounded on the metal. "Crawford, it's me. Honk or something if you're still alive."

I waited, then tried again. This time when there was no answer, I circled the tree, reached for the passenger's door handle and hauled myself up on the running board. The window was open. I looked inside and immediately wished I hadn't.

The state police showed up first, and a trooper questioned me until the ambulance arrived. Who was I to the deceased? Had I seen what caused him to go off the road?

Then I made the mistake of saying Crawford had been trying to run me over.

"Why would he do that?" asked the trooper.

"We had a dispute over some trash."

The events that followed were an unequivocal shit-storm. Crawford had been a respected volunteer fireman, and since his death occurred just days before the annual Fireman's Bazaar and parade, they added his hearse to the procession. Not wanting to be conspicuously absent, I went to the parade and had to endure the dirty looks of marching firemen. The way they stared at me made me wonder if those rifles they carried on their shoulders were actually loaded. As a further indignity, I went to the carnival that night to play my best game—the high striker—and the carny refused to give me the mallet.

Then, just as Dwight had predicted, I was issued a summons for "civil trespass" and "theft of service." There was also a charge of "malicious destruction of private property" because of the chainsaw incident. I hired a lawyer, but the judge—whom I learned later was a friend of Crawford's—found me guilty on all charges and sentenced me to pay a $1,000 fine and to do 200 hours of community service.

In a bit of revenge from beyond the grave, days before I had to start my community service I was diagnosed with Lyme disease. I'd gotten the tick bite when I went through the woods to try and save Crawford. Even with the antibiotics, I felt as though Crawford *had* run me over. I'm pretty sure that's irony.

Well, by now you've probably guessed what my community service entailed: picking up roadside trash. I know what you're waiting for. You're waiting to hear my tearful declaration of how much I regret having thrown my trash in Crawford's Dumpster, but here's the deal: this may turn out to be a major lucky break for me.

One evening after trash detail, I got a call from a New York literary agent. She'd been antiquing in Wellington the same weekend the *Sentinel* ran the following headline about me and Crawford:

Garbage Feud Leaves One Man Dead, Lands Another in Court

"It's a fascinating story," the agent said. "Garbage is a hot-button issue right now, and we could do a real page-turner about your experiences. Possibly a TV movie, too. Oh, and don't worry if you're not a writer. I have several ghosts I've worked with. But this window won't stay open for long. Check out my website and get in touch."

It turned out that she had made a million-dollar deal for an internet cat personality that included book, TV and Broadway musical rights. Then and there, I decided to do it. If she could get me a deal like she got that cat, I might never have to work again.

Incredible.

And all because of some garbage.

10

WELLINGTON TRIALS

Although Titania had done all of the work, somehow I was breathless, as though her vigorous exertions while straddling me had not only pounded the air out of my lungs, but somehow ruptured my diaphragm. A vague worry crept over me that I might never draw a deep breath again.

Filtering through the blinds, the midnight lights of Park Avenue striped her face. Her mouth bloomed into a self-satisfied smile. I caressed her waist, her hips, her thighs as solid as plaster walls, and when I looked up at her again, the smile was gone, replaced by her familiar impassivity.

"Titania," I said, "that was…incredible."

While I panted, Titania gathered her churned-up hair into a ponytail and secured it with a band.

"Well, I do enjoy being on top."

She sprawled on her back across the other half of the mattress. This California King of hers would fill my entire studio apartment in Gramercy. It was so big that in the darkness I couldn't make her out distinctly. I reached out and touched her damp cheek to reassure myself she was still there.

"And *this*," she said, "isn't even my best riding activity."

She clapped her hands and the lights switched on—a computer-controlled convenience throughout her apartment that, during sex, with her backside slapping mightily against me, had become confused and kept switching the lights on and off. Bouncing on top of me, she had burst into laughter while the room went light to dark to light around us.

Titania, her smooth face now dappled with perspiration, her Slavic eyes regarding me with curiosity, faced me on her side, propped up on an elbow. This was the first time I'd been able to imbibe the entire, glorious, prepossessing length of her, and it did not disappoint. Cheeks, jaw, neck, breasts, stomach, legs—nothing but drum-tight skin and supple, elongated muscle. Certainly her age—25, I surmised—was partly responsible, but it was more than that. It was as though she and gravity had dueled, and gravity lost.

While like all men I craved reaching climax with a woman, it was the post-coital moments like this that I secretly adored. Not for the cuddling or the emotional connection, but for the dreamy, romantic state they put me in, shepherding my thoughts toward love scenes and lovers in great literature: Sarah and Bendrix in *The End of the Affair*; Catherine Barkley and Lt. Henry in *A Farewell to Arms*; and, most of all, Anna and Vronsky in *Anna Karenina*—the modern, Pevear–Volokhonsky translation of which I'd recently finished.

Although less expurgated than the century-old Constance Garnett translation, the new one still suffered from the prevailing morals of Tolstoy's time. Simply put, it lacked sex. In scene after scene, Anna and Vronsky display these vague feelings of desire for each other, but you never see them engaged in anything more than a passionate embrace. While I understood the value of restraint in fiction, it would have been nice if Tolstoy had shown the two of them ravishing each other. Which made me wonder: who would have been on top? Vronsky, pounding an O-faced Anna into a nest of pillows? Or Anna, shaking her aristocratic raven hair, reveling in her dominant position astride an awestruck Vronsky? I and other inquisitive readers would never know.

"So"—Titania brushed my ribs with the back of her hand—"how would you like to see me ride something else?"

"Excuse me?"

"Hold on. Be right back."

Even nude, she walked out of the room with purpose, as though marching in uniform, her right hand beating a silent tempo against her thigh.

From across the apartment there was the faint sound of a refrigerator being opened. Bottles rattled, drawers thumped.

She called out, "Hey, you want some cherries?"

"Cherries? Okay."

I could only imagine the kinky collection of fruit and toys she was assembling for our next round. When she returned, her hands were behind her back.

"Think fast!"

A bulging plastic bag opened in midair, raining cherries down on my naked skin. I squirmed on the bed.

"Jesus, Titania, they're cold!"

"Gotcha!" She jumped up and down, smiling and clapping. The automatic lights flashed like a discotheque.

I scooped up handfuls of the cherries and put them in the bag. Titania swept some out of the way and plopped down next to me. She placed a brochure on my chest.

"What's this?" I asked.

"It's a chance for you to see me in my best riding activity. This weekend, upstate."

She brushed my bangs off my forehead. It had been a long time since a woman did that to me and was curiously exciting.

"Give me a sec. I need my glasses."

"Don't worry," she said, smacking my butt, "I like that you're older than me. If you weren't, I'd probably kill us both. My stamina is ridiculous."

"It's not because I'm older, my dear. It's because all I do is *read*. If you read as much as I, you'd be wearing them, too. And by the way, my *stamina* is more than up to the challenge."

She gave my loins a salacious glance. "We'll see. Read it."

I found my glasses in my suit jacket and slipped them on. The brochure was for something called "The Wellington Trials at Fox Hill." From the photos, I assumed it had to do with horses. There were half a dozen pictures of jacketed, helmeted riders on horseback, including one of Titania jumping a rock wall. I smiled to myself. The faint, smug smile on her lips—as though her winning the event were a fait accompli—was strikingly similar to how she'd looked when we met a week ago, at Campbell Apartment in Grand Central.

I was at a table having drinks with an out-of-town author when I noticed Titania studying me from the bar. More than studying, actually. Hunting. There was a rapacious glint in her eyes, and her clothes, elegant but simple, contributed to this feeling I had of being hunted: knee-high chestnut boots, form-fitting khaki trousers and a plain white blouse open one button shy of slutty. Notoriously slow at drawing conclusions, I hadn't put it together yet—about her clothes and the horseback riding, I mean.

She was still at the bar when I said goodnight to the author. I strolled over to her as casually as a man being scoped out can, and pointed at her highball glass.

"What's that you're drinking?"

"A Normandy," she said, smiling.

"As in the Invasion of?"

She snapped her fingers and wagged one at me. "World War Two, right? How's my history?"

"Not bad. What's in it?"

"It's a cocktail made with Calvados," she said. "That's an apple brandy from Northern France. Hence, a Normandy."

From her yawning blouse, her posture and her seeming insouciance, I deduced that she had been watching me all night with one purpose in mind—sex. I decided to call her out.

"Hmm...*hence*," I said. "I once read that women who use that word have insatiable sex drives. Is that true?"

"Stick around. You might find out."

I ordered two Normandys and sat on the empty stool next to hers.

"So what's your name?" I asked.

"Titania."

"Ah, Queen of the Fairies in *A Midsummer Night's Dream.*"

"Really, is she? Cool."

"I'm Peter. Peter Ford."

"'Peter, Peter, pumpkin eater; had a wife but couldn't keep her,'" she said. "I don't know the rest."

"Unfortunately, I do. 'He put her in a pumpkin shell; and there he kept her very well.'"

"Oh…you're *good.*" She winked and thrust a hand at me. "Titania Hammersley."

Fittingly for a woman with such a patrician-sounding name, her hand was meticulously manicured, the nails polished but flush with her fingertips. She surprised me by gripping my hand not with the typical feminine finger-shake, but with the clasp of someone closing on a house. By the time I thought to strengthen my own grip, she had let go and was sipping her cocktail.

"So, let's get down to it, shall we?" she said. "This is where we're supposed to tell each other what we do for a living. Well, I'll tell you what I do. Nothing. My father is rich—*ludicrously* rich—so my mother and I have never had to do a thing. She's one of the original mail-order brides, by the way. Point is, I could draw the max from a hundred ATMs every day and never make a dent. It's a little depressing, actually. There are *many* days when I wake up and have no idea what to do with myself.

"I have a few passions, but I won't share them with you until we know each other better. Far as the money goes, I fall asleep every night feeling guilty about it, and I'll tell you a secret." She leaned forward until the down on our cheeks touched. "For years, I've been stealing from my father—a few thousand at a time—and giving it to charities. Battered women's shelters mostly. What else? I travel a lot, not that there's any great virtue in that, and I love film noir. Or is it *films* noir? Whatever. How about you?"

"I'm a book editor," I said. "Literary fiction mostly."

"Hoping to discover the next Fitzgerald?"

"Something like that."

"And that woman…one of your authors?"

I was nonplussed.

"Body language." She drained her glass and held it out for the bartender, who whisked by and grabbed it. "That and the papers you were looking over. Couples don't do that, unless they're buying a house or getting a divorce. Are you involved with somebody?"

"Not really, no."

"What's this 'not really' crap? Relationship status is a binary. Either you are or you aren't."

"Fine. I'm not. You?"

"If I were, would I have waited around for you all night?"

"Okay, we're both available," I said. "What's next, exchange blood test results?"

Titania leaned back on her stool, appraising me. She nodded.

"How are your abs?"

"Pardon?"

"Your stomach, your abdominals. Do you have a six-pack or what?"

"Well, I don't have a gut, if that's what you mean."

"Stand up," she said, biting her lower lip. "Closer." She grabbed me by the belt and pulled. "Move your jacket out of the way."

I complied.

"Now," she said, "tighten your stomach as hard you can. I'm going to punch you a few times."

"This is crazy."

"*No*...this is durability testing." She smiled as if at an inside joke.

"All right."

Standing before her, holding my suit jacket open, I flexed my abs. A couple at a neighboring table watched as Titania crunched on an ice cube and delivered a few solid punches to the area just above my pelvis. Then she banged both fists into me at the same time.

"Are you done?" I asked.

"Almost." She opened her hands and thrust her palms rhythmically against my hips, moving down to my upper thighs, faster and faster.

"Those aren't my abs."

I was wondering what this was about when she delivered a climactic double-punch that knocked me backwards into my stool. The woman behind me huffed. Once I'd re-tucked my shirt and straightened my tie, I turned back to Titania.

"What was that for?"

"Nothing," she said. "Just curious."

"Well, did I pass?"

"Yes, the practice exam anyway." She handed the bartender a black Amex card and pointed at both our glasses. "I'm paying."

"Thank you," I said, taking out a pen. "We should probably exchange phone numbers before—"

"Oh, I'm not done with you yet. Not even close." The bill came. She grabbed the pen out of my hand, scribbled a signature and handed the pen back. "My place is on Park Avenue. Not far from here, actually. Care to see it?"

"Sure."

I tried to sound nonchalant, as if being picked up by gorgeous rich women were a regular occurrence for me, when in fact the prospect of going back to Titania's apartment had me so keyed up that my leg jerked involuntarily, whacking my shin against the brass rail. As I rubbed it, my breathing was ragged.

"Ready?" She took my hand and walked us downstairs. "Hey, interesting fact. Did you know that old mattresses weigh twice as much as when they're new? *Twice.* And guess where that extra weight comes from. Sweat, Peter. Sweat and dead skin." We exited onto Vanderbilt Avenue. Her fingers interlocked with mine. "Let's walk. It's just a few blocks uptown."

With her free hand, she raked her hair over her shoulder. She nudged me.

"So, here's the deal," she said stonily. "I just got a brand-new California King mattress. Whaddaya say we put some *sweat* into it?"

Titania was nudging me again, this time in my naked ribcage as we lay on her bed.

"What do you think?" she asked. "Like to come see me ride? I'm pretty awesome at it, and it's really quite fascinating if you've never seen it before. You haven't, have you?"

"No, never have."

"Think of it as a trial run for us," she said. "This is a big weekend for me. Delegates from the U.S. Equestrian Team will be there. If I do well, I could be going to London next summer. London, baby!" She flailed her arms.

"You don't need to convince me, Titania. I'd love to see you ride."

I placed a hand on her bare butt. Dear God, it was harder than a submarine hull.

"I'm beginning to like you," she said.

She plucked the stem off a cherry, popped the cherry in her mouth, rolled it around and spat the pit across the room. It ricocheted off the wall.

"Titania!"

"Come here, Peter, Peter, pumpkin eater."

At the breathiness in her voice, my groin tingled and stirred. I felt like Bilbo Baggins watching Smaug awaken. Titania climbed on top of me and pinned me down, her nipples skating across mine. She kissed the cherry into my mouth.

"Mmm, terrific," I said. "But I didn't think they were in season right now."

"Sweetie," she said, reaching for a fresh condom, "when you're rich, *everything's* in season."

———◆———

Although I'd had several authors from Wellington over the years, including a former editor pal turned bestselling mystery novelist, not one of them had deigned to invite me to so much as a cocktail party up here. Creeping through the village that Saturday morning in a rental car,

I passed a shiny aluminum diner and myriad antiques dealers and continued on through a hamlet mysteriously called Rabbitsville (although I didn't see a single rabbit to warrant the name). From there, I followed sandwich boards pointing to Fox Hill.

The road ribboned out in front of me, over rolling green hills and miles of black wooden fence. The sky was a soft summer blue. In the hollows, pockets of thin fog hovered over the grass. The whole countryside had a vaguely mystical aura, like Mr. Darcy's Derbyshire.

Most of the drive from Manhattan, however, had been tedious. Droning along the empty and wooded Taconic Parkway, still half-asleep, I had started to question the wisdom of traveling two hours upstate for a young woman with whom I had done nothing but have inordinate sex—and that only in her favored cowgirl position. To be fair, we *had* managed to squeeze in a few substantial conversations—about books (for a young woman of prodigious sexual appetites she was surprisingly well-read, Chekhov's stories being her favorites); about technology (she embraced the useful, citing her automatic lights and a robotic vacuum cleaner that perpetually crawled around the apartment); and about lifestyles (she adored simplicity bordering on the Spartan; every room in her apartment contained minimal furniture and absolutely *no* knickknacks)—but since those conversations invariably took place before or after sex, I considered them suspect, and not representative of how we would relate under less sybaritic circumstances. For that reason, the weekend was a test, or, as she had put it, "a trial run for us."

Of course there was a chance she'd tire of me by Sunday evening, but I doubted it. When we'd kissed goodbye Wednesday night at the clock in Grand Central, practically making out in the withering gaze of the information booth clerk, she had clung to me like someone to a tree in a hurricane, gushing about the upcoming competition, the recent good weather, the soggy spring and how it would affect the course, the wide assortment of obstacles she had to jump, her rival riders, her private cottage on the estate, and how much her parents were going to love me. We kissed one last time at the train doors.

"Just so you know," she said, putting her hand on my heart, "you're the only guy I've ever taken up there. The only one. *Ever.*"

The road began a long, steady climb, and in the field to my right, some riders trotted along the fence. When I reached the summit, a *Who's Who* of luxury cars and SUVs, intermingled with an ambulance and a Wellington police car, lined both shoulders of the road. I parked and followed other spectators, or guests of the riders I presumed, down a path between two fences, toward the warm-up area.

For early June, it was hot. Not even nine o'clock yet and easily 80 degrees. In a summer suit and pastel striped tie I was farcically overdressed compared to the people around me, but that was the brochure's fault. In the photos everyone looked as if they were at the Kentucky Derby, so I had dressed accordingly.

Out in the field, a rider approached a water jump, the horse cantering toward it at an angle. I consulted the map in the brochure Titania had given me. It showed this course—the cross-country course—as a giant loop, ending on the near side of a large copse of trees, and beginning on the far side. An observation tower rose above the trees. There were people at the top, barely visible. The path I was on between the fences passed the cool-down area. A pair of riders, male and female, approached each other at the fence line.

"Michael, how was she?"

He shook his head. "I pulled up at seventeen."

"Oh, I'm so sorry," the woman said.

"Yeah, it didn't feel right. I mean, she's fine, but…it's still pretty mushy out there."

"It is."

"You'd think that with all their money, they'd do something about the drainage," he said. "Anyway, how'd *you* do?"

"Pretty good, I think. No penalties anyway."

"At least Caprice isn't competing this year. Gone gun crazy, apparently. Spending all her time at the shooting club. What about Titania, has she ridden yet?"

"No. She's in the next grouping." The woman sighed. "Hopefully my time will hold up."

Hearing another competitor mention Titania gave me a sadistic feeling of pride. The others were clearly afraid of her.

The warm-up area sat in the shade of the trees. Four riders and their mounts trotted around a small field as family and spectators stood beside the fence. Even though she was wearing a helmet, I picked out Titania immediately. She sat taller and steadier in her saddle than the others, clucking her horse, a glistening deep chestnut, into a canter. She rode in lazy circles, her face fiercely concentrated, until she noticed me and beamed. Wheeling the horse around, she jumped off before coming to a complete stop and ran toward the fence. I didn't know whether spectators were allowed in the warm-up area, but when I saw the elation on Titania's face, I didn't care. I climbed over the fence, and she threw her arms around me and kissed me like we were alone in her Park Avenue bedroom. When she looked up at me, her eyes were soft and gleaming.

"You're here," she said.

"I am."

She tapped me on the behind with her riding crop.

"And fabulously overdressed. Do you ever *not* wear a suit?"

"Yeah?" I pinched the sleeve of her polo shirt. "What's this? I thought you'd be wearing one of those fancy jackets with an ascot."

"You mean a cravat. Silly, those are for *dressage*, which was yesterday, and which I kicked ass in, by the way."

"Jolly good show," I said.

"Dork." With a quick glance over her shoulder, she sprang up on her tiptoes and spoke hotly in my ear. "I want to show you the stables after. There's a certain pile of hay with our names on it." She kissed me again. "Gotta go. Wish me luck."

A man boosted her into the saddle.

"Good luck," I said. "Where do I go now?"

"The tower," she said. "My parents and the other sponsors are up there, along with some of the delegates. Best view of the course. See you in half an hour, baby!"

Before I could get her parents' names, she trotted away to the far end of the field, stopping the horse several yards away from the other riders. I found the tower and climbed the stairs—four flights of them—pausing on the final landing to dab my face with my pocket square. Then I took a deep breath, forced a smile and continued to the top.

Three couples stood at the rails, along with a man and two women in matching crested jackets and straw plantation hats—the equestrian team delegates, I reasoned. A woman in an event uniform handed me a pair of binoculars and a glass of champagne.

"Who is your party, sir?"

"I'm with Titania Hammersley," I said.

A tall balding man with tufts of white hair on either side of his head swung around from the railing and eyed me superciliously. He tapped the arm of a woman beside him.

"The boyfriend," he said.

The woman was a dark brunette with alabaster skin. At first I saw her only in profile, and was enchanted by her fine features, but when she turned to face me—and face me she did with her cool Slavic eyes—I felt as though I were seeing a living incarnation of Anna Karenina.

"Ah, yes," she said. "The book editor."

"It's a pleasure to meet you both," I said. "Peter Ford."

"John."

"Natasha."

I shook hands with them.

"May I join you?" I asked.

"Certainly." John stepped aside, creating space between him and his wife. "Titania's first in her group. Should be starting any minute."

"I've been looking forward to seeing her ride," I said.

"These books you edit. What is the genre?" Natasha asked.

Her accent was noticeable. Titania had told me that her mother was one of the original Russian mail-order brides, but until I heard Natasha speak, the fact hadn't fully registered with me.

"Fiction," I said. "Literary."

"This includes romance, yes?"

"Yes, Natasha. Some."

John's eyes flashed. "What, no non-fiction?" He threw his arms up, apparently forgetting he was holding a glass of champagne. Half of it went over the railing.

"Well…yes," I said, "a bit."

"How about ghostwriters? Know any? I was thinking of doing a book myself."

"Oh? What about?"

"You know, this and that. My philanthropy. Life lessons I've learned. Business deals, that sort of thing."

I sipped some champagne. "If you don't mind my asking, sir, how did you earn your fortune?"

"Well, it's inherited mostly," he said. "Tungsten."

"Excuse me, sir, did you say, 'tungsten'?"

He nodded crisply. "For light bulb filaments."

Natasha gazed out at the fields. Watching her, it was easy for me to see where Titania got her statuesque looks.

"I read many Danielle Steele," Natasha said. "You could get me autograph?"

"I don't know her personally," I said, "but—"

An announcement blared over the loudspeaker: *Next up on the cross-country course, Wellington's own Titania Hammersley, riding her gelding, Gurov.*

I smiled at this homage of hers to the Chekhov character. The announcer continued.

"After her flawless showing in dressage yesterday, Miss Hammersley goes into today's competition well ahead of the field. Titania Hammersley, number nine, starts now."

I put down my champagne and trained the binoculars on the starting area.

"How much do these ghostwriters charge?" John asked.

"It varies, sir, but for a good one, which you'd want, I'd say fifty thousand."

"What? So, what kind of advance could I expect?"

"That's hard to say."

"Well, we can discuss this later," he said.

After some frantic searching with the binoculars, I found Titania and got her in focus. A buzzer sounded over the loudspeaker. She took off.

The first half dozen obstacles, either plain wooden jumps or adorned with flowers, she and Gurov cleared easily, sailing over them and landing catlike on the turf with distance to spare. Once Titania successfully jumped a hedge-topped rock wall, she leaned forward gripping Gurov's mane and whipped him into a full-blown gallop. Mud kicked up behind them.

"There she goes," the proud father said, rapping on the wooden rail. "It's a done deal at this point."

We crossed to the other side of the tower.

"I never see her so relaxed," Natasha said. "What has relaxed her so?"

Out of the corner of my eye, I noticed Natasha lower her binoculars and look me up and down. I continued to peer out at the course.

Of the next seven obstacles, only three were visible from the tower—a dry ditch behind a grassy mound, a water-filled ditch, and two rail fences in close succession—and to my untrained eye she executed them flawlessly. Then she careened down a steep hill and out of sight. An equestrian dead zone. Like a spacecraft during reentry.

"She'll come out over there." John Hammersley pointed at a wooden wall built into a gap in a hedgerow. "Five feet high. Toughest obstacle on the course. After that, she'll be home free."

I zoomed in on the wall. Two small signs—one red, one white—formed guideposts for the wall, so the wall could be distinguished from the greenery of the hedgerow. The white signs had numbers on them: 17. I thought of the rider's comment earlier—that he had pulled up at number 17—and in barely the amount of time it took for me to gasp a breath, I was staggered by a sense of literary déjà vu: Vronsky's disaster in the steeplechase! I ran down the tower stairs.

By the time the announcement came over the loudspeaker, I had climbed over a fence and was sprinting across the field to her.

———◆•◆•◆———

When I reached her, she was hopping on one leg in a huge mud puddle, clutching the reins against the saddle, trying to remount the horse. One entire side of her was brown with mud, the other side clean. Tears streaked her face.

"Damn it, Gurov, stand still!" She whipped the horse shockingly hard across the shoulder and jerked on the reins. Then she saw me.

"Help me! I have to finish, I have to finish!"

Wrapping an arm around her, I took the reins and shooed the horse away.

"Get him back!" Titania shouted. "I have to finish!"

A siren wailed in the distance.

"I have to finish!" She hugged my neck and began to bawl.

The nearest hospital was in Sharon, Connecticut, just over the state line. The paramedics applied a splint to her leg, and then, believing I was her husband, let me ride in back. They administered a drip of something that quieted her. I think the paramedic called it "fentanyl." Whatever it was, it threw a switch in her: she stopped crying and instead stared blankly at me. She spoke as if I were a figment of her dreams.

"'Peter, Peter, pumpkin eater; had a wife but couldn't keep her,'" she said. "*Why* couldn't you keep her, Peter?"

"Shhh."

"You needed a pumpkin shell, right?"

"That's right."

My hand trembled as I stroked her forehead. The ambulance siren squawked and bleeped, and we passed a few cars. They shrank in the back windows.

"Who was she, Peter?"

"A mistake, that's all."

"What happened?"

"She expected it to be easier," I said. "She lacked your character, your toughness. I'll tell you more later."

"I *am* tough, aren't I, Peter?"

"Yes you are. And sexy. And talented. And smart."

"And *rich*. Don't forget rich, baby."

The paramedic riding in back with us smiled over her paperback.

"That doesn't matter to me," I said.

"I know, but it does to me." She wormed a hand out from beneath the blanket and held mine. "You liked seeing me ride?"

"I did. Very much."

"I would have won, you know."

"Yes, and next year you will."

"Next year," she scoffed. "Try next *month*. I'm going to the Olympics, mister." She squeezed my hand. "Gurov—is he okay?"

"He's fine."

"I shouldn't have whipped him."

"He'll forgive you."

Titania lifted her head and glanced at her leg. "Seems I won't be on top for a while." She blinked at me.

"Good," I said, tucking the blanket around her neck. "Now I finally get a chance to show what Peter Ford can do."

"Ha, we'll see."

I held my hand against her cheek. She smiled at me. "Peter?"

"Yes?"

She beckoned me close. As I leaned over her, she lifted her head off the pillow and whispered in my ear.

"I think I love you."

THE END

ABOUT THE AUTHOR

Chris Orcutt has written professionally for over 20 years as a fiction writer, journalist, scriptwriter, playwright, technical writer and speechwriter.

Orcutt is the creator of the critically acclaimed Dakota Stevens Mystery Series, including *A Real Piece of Work* (#1), *The Rich Are Different* (#2) and *A Truth Stranger Than Fiction* (#3). Orcutt's short story collection, *The Man, The Myth, The Legend*, was voted by IndieReader as one of the best books of 2013. And his modern pastoral novel *One Hundred Miles from Manhattan* (an IndieReader Best Book for 2014) prompted *Kirkus Reviews* to favorably compare Orcutt to Pulitzer Prize-winning author John Cheever.

As a newspaper reporter Orcutt received a New York Press Association award, and while an adjunct lecturer in writing for the City University of New York, he received the Distinguished Teaching Award.

If you would like to contact Chris, you can email him at corcutt007@yahoo.com or tweet him @chrisorcutt. For more information about Orcutt and his writing, or to follow his blog, visit his website: www.orcutt.net.

EXCERPT FROM
THE MAN, THE MYTH, THE LEGEND

Chris Orcutt's short story collection *The Man, The Myth, The Legend* was voted by IndieReader as one of the Best Indie Books of 2013. This collection of entertaining and unique stories explores the worlds of 10 very different men, ranging from a safari big-game hunter to a bootlegger to a speechwriter. Following is the opening from the lead-off story in the collection, "The Last Great White Hunter."

His name was Buck Remington, and with a name like that he was destined to become one of the greatest Great White Hunters in Africa. Among his female clients he was known by another name, but how Buck earned that moniker is the subject of an infamous unauthorized biography and will not be discussed here.

So, what kind of a man was he? More than a man's man, that's for sure.

He was a man's man's man.

Stronger and more virile than a dozen of today's video game-playing punks, even at age 85 when he undertook his last safari Buck Remington made Clint Eastwood and Anthony Quinn look like towel boys in a Turkish bathhouse. He never lost a bar fight or a poetry quoting or drinking contest. Nairobi swam in his illegitimate offspring—the sons and daughters of cooks and seamstresses, heiresses and plantation owners. As for his own history, it was as though he'd been born in the savanna and raised by lions. He spoke a polyglot of American and British English, with a smattering of Swahili picked up in the bush, leading some to believe he was the orphaned son of an American industrialist or, like Tarzan, the descendant of a long-lost member of the Peerage. In the 1980s there was talk of his being knighted, but when neither Buck's birthplace nor his citizenship could be proved, the matter was quietly dropped.

His long and storied career began when he was but 9 years old (he looked 16) as an assistant to legendary English hunter Philip Percival, on the maiden safari of American writer Ernest Hemingway. Observing Buck's innate, highly developed skills of tracking and shooting, and his extraordinary "grace under pressure," as Hemingway called it, both men predicted a bright future for the boy hunter.

To lesser men, Buck's 76-year career had been a smashing success, but his accomplishments were not enough to douse the fires of ambition that burned hotter in him than a South African dry season. In fact he considered himself a jackal of a failure, having bagged only 162 rhino, 217 elephant, 496 lion, 375 Bengal tiger, 306 antelope (fast buggers), 285 cheetah, 609 Cape buffalo, 531 kudu, 439 leopard, countless hyena (stopped counting after 900), 55 crocodiles, 16 hippo (self-defense), a savage thieving baboon, and a handful of wild dogs, shot for practice from a moving truck.

It was reflecting on these paltry numbers that caused Buck Remington to rise from bed more slowly than usual on the morning of his final safari. His bed mate was an American divorcee who had been inspired to travel the world after reading that *Eat, Pray, Love* bollocks. He slapped her backside.

"Time to go, my dear."

"One more time, Buck. Please?"

"Sorry, love. Meet my clients in three-quarters of an hour, and I haven't breakfasted yet. Breakfast for one, I'm afraid."

He called downstairs and ordered his usual be brought up. The door clicked shut when the woman left. He retrieved his revolver, a Freedom Arms Model 83, from beneath the pillow and holstered it. Chambered for .475 Linebaugh, it made a .44 magnum seem like a child's cap gun. It could stop a charging lion dead at 20 feet and had deterred more than a few jealous husbands.

Buck was at the sink, shaving with the straight razor he had once used to cut a lion's throat, when breakfast arrived: steak & eggs, toast with marmalade, a pot of black Kenyan coffee, and a very stiff Bloody Mary (one needed one's vegetables). He sawed into the rare beef, sipped the coffee, quaffed the hair of the dog. His houseboy entered with his jacket and hat.

"Lucky jacket, Bwana."

"Good. Hang it up there."

Buck finished his breakfast, checked the time and went to the bush jacket. It was the last of two dozen a client had given him long ago, back when Abercrombie & Fitch was a high-end outfitter, before they became a purveyor of snug undershirts for sexually confused teenagers. For a moment he stood in the light from the window, admiring the good stout twill, the reinforced elbows like rhino hide, the elastic loops holding the obscene cartridges for his Holland and Holland .600NE double rifle. Looked like shells for a bloody flak gun. The pockets contained the essentials: a dozen extra .475 shells, two packs of Chesterfields, matches, and a flask of Macallan 18-year.

As he removed the jacket from its hanger and slipped it on, he glanced at himself in the mirror. Freshly shaved, tanned and with his full head of hair, Buck routinely passed for a brisk man of 50 among his female clients and the patronesses of hotel bars around the world. Today, however, he didn't feel young. Today he was overcome by a sense of finality. He knew he wouldn't be coming back from this safari. How that old bastard Death would finally get him—shot in the head by his client, impaled on a rhino horn, mauled in the brush trying to finish off a wounded leopard—he had no idea. He only hoped it would be worthy of the life he'd lived as a great hunter and not something undignified, like what had happened to his old rival, Richards. A decade later, and Buck still couldn't think about it...